Beautiful
DEMONS

PEACHVILLE HIGH DEMONS
BOOK 1

SARRA CANNON

Cover Design by Robin Ludwig Design, Inc.
Editing Services by Janet Bessey at Dragonfly Editing
Formatting by Inkstain Interior Book Designing
www.InkstainFormatting.com

BOOKS BY SARRA CANNON:

YOUNG ADULT

PEACHVILLE HIGH DEMONS SERIES:

Beautiful Demons
Inner Demons
Bitter Demons
Shadow Demons
Rival Demons
Demons Forever

A Demon's Wrath: Part 1
A Demon's Wrath: Part 2

ETERNAL SORROWS SERIES:

Death's Awakening
Sorrow's Gift

NEW ADULT

FAIRHOPE SERIES:

The Trouble With Goodbye
The Moment We Began
A Season For Hope
The Fear Of Letting Go

Sacrifice Me

—To all of the Beautiful Demons out there.
Thank you for taking a chance on me.

THIS IS YOUR
LAST CHANCE

*S*IX FOSTER HOMES in one year had to be some kind of record. I ran my sapphire pendant along the silver chain around my neck and looked out at the pine trees zooming past. Where would they send me next?

"I don't know what got into you, Harper," Mrs. Meeks said. Her hair shot out every which way and she wasn't wearing any makeup. The call to come pick me up probably came in after she'd gone to bed for the night. "I can't keep doing this."

I eyed her. Was she passing me off to another case worker? Mrs. Meeks had been there with me from the beginning. Since the fire. I didn't want her to abandon me now.

"It was an accident," I said. I sat up straight in my seat and studied her tired face. I needed her to believe me.

"An accident?" Her voice took on the shrill tone I had come to expect from her. "Mrs. Sanders said you threw a lamp at her. How could that have been an accident, Harper?"

"I didn't exactly throw it," I said. I bit my lip. How could I possibly explain it to Mrs. Meeks? Or anyone for that matter?

One second I was arguing with Mrs. Sanders about a party she wouldn't let me go to and the next, well, everything in the room that wasn't nailed down was floating three inches in the air. "It just sort of-"

"Sort of what? Threw itself?" Her face contorted into an angry grimace. She didn't believe me.

I sank into the leather seat and sighed. No one ever believed me. Instead, they called me names like 'witch' and 'freak'.

"Harper," she said, her voice softening. "I've always tried to place you in the very best foster homes in the city. Places where I thought they would try to understand your..." She searched for the word. "Your unique issues. But this is the sixth foster home you've been kicked out of this year. And with your history." She glanced over at me and sighed heavily. "It's getting harder and harder to place you."

My history.

I leaned my forehead against the window and felt the cool glass against my skin. After everything I'd done, it made sense that no one wanted me. I closed my eyes and remembered the beautiful porcelain skin of my adopted mother, Jill. I never meant to hurt anyone, especially not her.

"At this point, there's no other choice," Mrs. Meeks said.

I opened my eyes and looked over at her. In the light from the dashboard, she looked old. Worried. Angry. A wave of nausea rolled over me.

"No other choice than what?"

She looked over and patted my leg with her hand. Not a good sign.

"I'm taking you to a place called Shadowford Home," she said. "It's in a town south of here. Peachville. And the woman who runs it is well known for taking in girls who are struggling in the regular system. Girls like you."

There are no girls like me, I thought. "I've never heard of it."

"Peachville is a small community. Very different from Atlanta. I think it'll be a good place for you. Atlanta is just too big. Too full of opportunities to get in trouble or get mixed up with the wrong crowd." She pulled the car off the interstate. From the looks of it, we were in the middle of nowhere. "But I have to be completely honest with you, Harper. If you can't make it work at Shadowford, I'll have no choice but to take you to juvenile detention until you turn eighteen."

I sat up. "What? You can't be serious."

A home for troubled girls was bad enough. I certainly didn't belong in juvie. I'd known people who had gone to the one in Atlanta. It was practically like prison for teens. Constant supervision. No freedom. Strict rules. My entire body tensed just thinking about it.

"What did you expect?" she said. "Since you were eight years old, I've placed you in foster home after foster home, and you've been nothing but trouble for these families. Throwing lamps. Breaking windows. Fires."

"None of those things were my fault," I said. Anger and frustration stirred deep in my stomach. How dare she bring up the fire. I had only been eight when that happened, and it wasn't my fault. It wasn't!

Change rattled in the cup holder that sat between us in the car. Quickly, I slammed my hand down over the top of it.

Not now.

Mrs. Meeks continued on, thankfully not noticing the rattling noise. "It's time you learned to take responsibility for your actions," she said. "Make things work at Shadowford or you'll go to juvenile detention for the next two years. I'm sorry, but this is your last chance, Harper."

DO NOT TOUCH
MY THINGS

*W*E SPENT THE night in a hotel just off the interstate. First thing in the morning, we were back out on the road, heading to Peachville, Georgia. I had never lived in a small town before. Or a group home for that matter.

The light was shining through the thick pine trees as we turned down an unmarked gravel road an hour later. "We should be close," Mrs. Meeks said.

A large, weather-worn sign that read "Shadowford Plantation" came into view. I sat up straight and peered through the dense trees. A winding red dirt road led back to a clearing. Mrs. Meeks stopped the car at the top of the hill and we both stared open-mouthed at the huge white plantation house below.

Shadowford stood three stories tall with long white columns running from the roof to the wraparound porch. Paint flaked off the white walls and green ivy blanketed the sides of the porch, as if nature was slowly reclaiming the house for itself. Centered on the second floor level was a large balcony with a wrought-iron railing. A girl with bright red hair stood on the balcony. She waved toward us, then disappeared into the house.

As we drove the rest of the road up to the house, a chill ran down my spine. There was something different about this place I couldn't quite put my finger on. The house itself, though old, was breathtaking. But there was also something dark about it. Unsettling. The house grew slowly larger, and my stomach lurched. I wanted to tell Mrs. Meeks to turn around and take me back to Atlanta. To juvenile detention if that was the only option. This house was... what?

Evil.

The word popped into my head and I shivered. That was ridiculous. A house couldn't be evil. It was just my nerves getting to me.

A pretty middle-aged woman stepped out onto the porch. She wore a faded blue dress and her brown hair was piled high in a messy bun at the top of her head. When I looked up at her, she smiled. Her dark eyes were warm and kind, immediately putting me at ease. I realized I'd been holding my breath, and I exhaled. Maybe I had only imagined the creepy aura around this place. Maybe everything was going to be alright.

I stepped out of the car and grabbed my bag from the backseat.

"You must be Harper," the woman said. She walked over and gave me a gentle hug. "We're so happy to have you here at Shadowford."

"Thanks."

"I'm Ella Mae Hunt. I help Mrs. Shadowford out quite a bit, so we'll be gettin' to know each other pretty well." She had a lilting southern accent that was sweet and gentle.

Ella Mae took my bag and set it just outside the front door. "I'll give you a few minutes to say goodbye, and then I'll take you inside and introduce you to our other girls."

I walked over to Mrs. Meeks and she gave me a big hug. "I'm sorry," I said.

"Everything could be different for you here," she said. "Treat this like a fresh start. A clean slate."

I squeezed her back briefly, then let go. Maybe she was right and things really could be different here. A new school in a new town. No one here knew my history.

"I'll do my best," I told her.

"I know you will."

With a sad smile, she got in her car and drove away. I watched until she disappeared from sight, then turned to my new home. Ella Mae was waiting for me by the front door.

"I think you'll really like it here," she said, opening the door to the big house. "Girls, come on down here and meet Harper."

Ella Mae's voice echoed through the high ceilings of the front hallway. Honey-colored wood floors shone beneath her feet and a large staircase rose up to the second floor landing. Three girls made their way down to us.

"This is Courtney James," Ella Mae said. A tall girl who looked to be slightly younger than me stepped forward and held her hand out to me. Her long, straight blond hair lay over her face, covering nearly the entire left side. She kept her head down, her eyes on the floor. When I touched her hand, it was ice cold and limp.

"I'm Agnes." The redheaded girl I'd seen on the balcony stepped out from behind Courtney and gave me a big welcoming hug. Her eyes were light green and she seemed to smile from within. I liked her immediately. "You'll be in the room next to mine," she said. "I'm so excited to have another house-mate here, you have no idea. Where are you coming from?"

"Atlanta."

"Oh cool, I've never been to Atlanta. In fact, Peachville's even bigger than the crappy town where I was born, and believe me, that's saying a lot."

I laughed. Her bubbly attitude was contagious and I felt all of the anxiety about the house begin to fade away.

"This is Mary Anne Marsters," she said, pulling me over to meet the third girl who was still standing on the bottom step. "She doesn't really talk much."

Mary Anne was obviously younger than the rest of us. I'd guess she was about thirteen or so. Her short black hair was tucked behind her ears and her pale skin was flawless. I reached my hand out to her, but she merely stared at it for a second, then turned around and walked back up the stairs.

"Don't mind her," Agnes said. "It takes her some time to get used to people."

Ella Mae picked up my tattered bag and handed it to Agnes. "Take this up to Harper's room now, would you Agnes? I'm going to take her in to meet Mrs. Shadowford. I'll send her upstairs in a few minutes and you can show her around."

"Sure thing," Agnes said, then bounded up the stairs two at a time.

I wondered why Mrs. Shadowford hadn't met us out front, but when I entered her dark, lush office, I understood right away. She was in a wheelchair. An older woman, she had shockingly white hair that ran in a single braid pulled over her shoulder. Her pale blue eyes seemed to pierce through me as she turned and sized me up. Butterflies danced around in my belly. This woman was unlike anyone I had ever met before. She had an energy about her that was strong and powerful. I knew right away that she was not the kind of person I wanted to cross.

"Harper Madison," she said. She studied me for a long moment, her eyes squinted and her lips pursed together in a tight, thin line. "I hear you've had some trouble in the past with both your adopted parents and several foster homes."

"Yes, ma'am." My voice trembled a bit, betraying my fear. I shifted my weight from one foot to another and studied the thick, patterned rug on the floor.

"It's no surprise that no one else wants you."

Her words stung. I wondered if I'd even heard her right.

"You're damaged. A broken girl," she said. "And some of the things you've done to the people taking care of you? Well, some of those things are unspeakable."

My face grew hot. Yes, some of the things I had done were terrible. Someone was dead because of me. I had to carry that guilt with me everywhere, but no one had ever said it out loud like that. The tone of her voice was bitter and cold, like she believed I had done those things on purpose. I opened my mouth to defend myself, but the look in her eyes stopped me.

"I don't want to hear your excuses."

"I never meant to hurt anyone." I stepped forward, putting my hand on the mahogany desk that separated us.

"Do not touch my things," Mrs. Shadowford said through gritted teeth. Her eyes grew wide and intense. I pulled my hand back quickly, but I could see that I'd made the old woman angry. On the desk, her tea cup rattled in its saucer. She reached out quickly to still the cup and the room grew silent. Fear gripped my chest, making it hard to breathe.

The air in the small office grew thick and warm. Mrs. Shadowford cleared her throat, then took her hand off the small cup. "That's enough for this morning. Ella Mae will take you through the house rules."

I stepped away from Mrs. Shadowford's desk slowly, then turned to leave the room. My hand closed around the cold brass knob of the door and a small shock of electricity went through my body. I yanked my hand back, surprised.

"Harper," Mrs. Shadowford said from her spot behind the desk.

My body tensed as I turned to find her blue eyes staring straight into mine. I tried to swallow, but my mouth had gone completely dry. "Yes ma'am?"

"I'll be watching you."

TROUBLE ALWAYS FINDS ME

"THE RULES ARE as follows. No back talk or disrespect, especially when it comes to the staff. You will need to keep your grades up at Peachville High. We expect to see A's and B's only. If any of your test grades are lower than a B, you'll need to bring them home for one of us to sign."

Ella Mae went on to list rules that were pretty common for foster homes. Lights out at eleven. No boys allowed upstairs. Keep your hands to yourself. Don't take anything that doesn't belong to you. All standard rules. Then, as if it were just another rule, she said, "And never, under any circumstances, are you to go up to the third floor."

Immediately, a strange tingle went through my body. If she had never mentioned it, I probably wouldn't have given the third floor a second thought. But now it was mysterious. Forbidden. Tempting. What could they possibly be hiding up there that would be so important to protect?

"Let me be completely clear about this. If you are found breaking any of the rules we've talked about today, you'll be expelled from Shadowford without a second chance. Do you understand?"

I nodded.

"And from what your case manager said on the phone when she called last night, you'll go straight from here to the detention center in Atlanta. You seem like such a sweet girl. I would hate to see you end up at a place like that."

I didn't want to see myself end up there either. Juvenile detention was like a jail sentence. Not to mention that going there for my last few years of high school would kill my chances at ever getting into a good college. I had to make things work here, no matter what. That meant putting whatever was up on the third floor out of my mind. Not to mention whatever had happened with Mrs. Shadowford's teacup. I told myself it was nothing – that it couldn't be the same thing that happened to me when I got angry – then followed Ella Mae through the first floor of the house.

Shadowford was even bigger than it looked from the outside. The large staircase split the floor in half. On one side was a formal sitting room with a big brick and tile fireplace. Heavy gold drapes hung in the windows and the antique furniture looked ornate and expensive. Ella Mae told me that the sitting room was only used for formal meetings and sometimes for special occasions.

Behind the sitting room was a formal dining room that held a long, shiny table and ten matching chairs. Against the wall, a china cabinet held beautiful bone china, crystal champagne flutes and silver serving trays. A sparkling chandelier hung above the table and a pretty stained glass window sent colorful light dancing across the room.

"Is this where we'll eat every day?" I asked. I had never even been in a room so immaculate and fancy. If I had to eat here, I'd be scared of messing something up.

"No. Usually we all eat at the table in the kitchen. It's a little more casual and laid back in there. But on nights when Mrs. Shadowford joins us, she prefers us to eat in the dining room."

I wondered how often that actually happened. Hopefully not very often. The old woman completely creeped me out. If at all possible, I planned to avoid her.

The kitchen ran along the back of the house. It was a huge room with lots of large windows that bathed the room in natural light. A large oak table with a scarred top and six mismatched chairs took up a large part of the floor on one side, while the other side held the main area of the kitchen. The cabinets were painted a buttery yellow that gave the whole room a happy, cheerful feeling. So far, it was my favorite room in the house.

"Sharon Griffith is our cook here. Sharon, this is Harper, our newest resident."

Sharon was a tall, pudgy woman with super short brown hair. She was cleaning the countertops and barely looked up to nod a curt hello to me. I had never had an actual cook before. At several of the foster homes, I'd been expected to fix my own meals most of the time.

The final room Ella Mae brought me into was warm and inviting. "This is where the girls like to hang out and study or watch TV," she said.

The leather couch in the center of the room looked comfortable and worn. Fuzzy blankets were piled together in a basket in the corner. Books were arranged neatly on built-in bookcases on either side of the flat panel TV. I glanced through the titles and saw a few that actually looked interesting.

A couple of worn desks lined the room on the left side, each holding a cup of pencils, a stack of blank paper, and a laptop. "Can anyone use the computers?"

"We only have those two laptops and anyone is free to use them as long as they stay down here in this room at all times.

There is wireless internet, but you have to get permission to use it," she said.

I sighed. At least there was some link to the outside world here, but it would be a pain to get permission to use the internet every time. I'm sure all my friends in Atlanta would be wondering what the heck happened to me. They'd all get to school Monday and find out that I was moved to another town. Hopefully, no one would know exactly what happened. I'd have to think up something good for the email I sent out, but I could worry about that later.

The rest of the rooms on the first floor made up Mrs. Shadowford's private suite. "Unless you're specifically invited to go inside, those rooms are strictly off limits."

Finally, Ella Mae led me up the stairs, down the hallway, and into a pretty room with light blue walls. "This will be your room," she said.

I stepped inside and my mouth opened in awe. A queen sized wooden bed with a beautiful canopy was the centerpiece of the room. On one wall there was a dressing table with a beautiful mirror attached and a stool to sit on. The floors were covered in the middle by a plush rug in dark blue. "Are all the rooms like this?"

Ella Mae laughed and touched my arm gently. "This is a gorgeous old house. I know you're going to love it here. Mrs. Shadowford is really a wonderful, giving woman once you get to know her. And she's so generous, letting you girls use this heirloom furniture that's been in her family for generations. I trust that you'll treat these things with care and respect."

Wonderful and giving weren't the first words that came to mind when I thought about the woman I'd met downstairs, but Ella Mae had a point. No one had ever trusted me with such opulent, expensive things. It only made it all the more important that I didn't mess up and let my anger get the best of me here.

SARRA CANNON

"Hi neighbor," Agnes said, knocking three times on my door. "What do you think? These rooms are amazing aren't they?"

"I'll leave you two girls to get acquainted," Ella Mae said. "See you downstairs in an hour for lunch, then we'll head into town to get supplies for school Monday."

When we were alone, Agnes plopped onto my bed. "Don't you just love this canopy? I have one in my room too, but it's red instead of blue. And did you see your bathroom?"

I shook my head and she jumped up and went to a closed door on the other side of the bed. When she opened it, I could hardly believe my eyes. "Are you serious?"

In a house with three other girls, I fully expected to share a bathroom. Instead, I had this large bathroom with a claw-foot tub and the cutest white pedestal sink all to myself.

"Totally. Each of us gets our own bathroom here, which is way cool," she said. "We're responsible for cleaning our own rooms and bathrooms at least once a week. And we have to do our own laundry and stuff. I don't care, though. This is by far the nicest place I've ever lived."

"How long have you been here?" We walked back into my main room and I started unpacking my bag. I didn't have much. Just a few torn pairs of jeans, some t-shirts, and other essentials. My sapphire necklace was pretty much the only thing of value that I had.

"Oh gosh. Almost two years, I guess. Ever since I was fourteen."

I continued to unpack as Agnes talked about the school and the town and how different things had been for her ever since she first came to Shadowford. She talked about this place as though it had saved her life. I couldn't help but wonder if it would do the same for me.

When my clothes and things were put away, I stuffed my bag under the bed and walked over to the window to see what

14

kind of view I had from up here. My room faced the back of the house. Just behind where the kitchen was, a cement patio extended outward. Agnes said that sometimes they had barbeque's out back there. Beyond the patio was a garden, and although it looked overgrown, it was still filled with a mixture of colorful flowers and leafy plants. A stone fountain in the middle was covered with deep green moss. Many years ago, it must have been so beautiful out there, but now it was neglected and almost eerily dark.

"What are those buildings out back? Past the garden?"

Agnes peered around me and squinted in the bright sunlight. "Well, the building there off to the right of the house is the barn. I've never been in there, but I guess there's like tools and stuff in there. And back behind the garden is the house where Ella Mae lives."

Movement near the barn caught my eye, and I saw someone quickly dart out from behind the weathered brown door. When he turned around, my heart did a little double time. It was a guy who looked about my age, maybe a little bit older, and he was gorgeous. He wore a plain black t-shirt and loose jeans, torn at the knee. His hair was brown and spiked up a bit on top. He looked like the kind of guy who didn't follow the rules. Even from this distance, I could tell he was tall.

"I thought there were no boys here," I said, nodding toward the guy. He glanced around as if to make sure no one had seen him come out of the barn, then started walking toward the house.

"Oh him," Agnes said. "That's Ella Mae's son, Jackson. Trust me when I say you don't want anything to do with him."

"Why not?"

"He's trouble."

As if to prove her point, Jackson stopped and looked straight up at me. My face flushed as our eyes met across the distance. Casually, he raised his hand to shield his eyes from the mid-morning sun. Yes, he was trouble alright. No matter where I went, trouble always seemed to find me.

I waved down to him and Jackson's face broke out in a smile. He lifted his chin in a nod of acknowledgment, then turned and made his way back to the small house behind the garden.

GUYS LIKE DRAKE ONLY DATE CHEERLEADERS

"COME ON," AGNES said, taking my hand. "Let's go down to Lori's and look around. I'll help you pick out stuff for school."

Downtown Peachville was so not what I was expecting. I thought it would be full of rundown brick buildings, empty storefronts, maybe an occasional pickup truck. Instead, the town was immaculate with red brick sidewalks, lush green trees planted along the road, fresh paint in pretty pastels, and thriving businesses. Ella Mae drove the four of us girls into town in a big white cargo van that said "Shadowford Home for Girls" on the side. I was glad to get away from the huge advertisement that basically told any of my future classmates that I was a troubled orphan.

Courtney disappeared into a consignment shop called "Second Beauty" and Mary Anne followed Ella Mae to the grocery store, sticking close by her side the whole time. Agnes dragged me past a drug store, a photography studio, and a clothing shop until we got to Lori's, a bigger store full of pretty things like candles, cards, and nick-knacks.

"This is my favorite store in town." She pulled open the front door and a little bell jingled. A cute woman up front with pigtails and blue ribbons in her hair waved and said hello. "Hi Lori," Agnes called. "Lori used to be one of the head cheerleaders for the Peachville Demons. She's so pretty isn't she? This is always the first store I come to when we get some time in town."

It was going to take some time to get used to having someone like Agnes to talk to all the time. It had been a long time since I'd lived with anyone I cared to talk to for more than a few minutes.

"I like it," I said, running my hand across a row of beaded purses on the table. "But what can I get here for school? It's not like I need a purse or anything."

Agnes led me over to the backpacks and school supplies. "Here, pick out anything you need. I'm gonna go over to the candles and look around for a few. You okay over here by yourself?"

I smiled. "Yeah, I think I've got it under control."

She practically bounced over to the other side of the store leaving me in the back section alone. I picked through the backpacks. The foster home I'd been in last had insisted I leave all of my school stuff with them since they paid for it. A lot of times, at a new place, I'd end up with someone's hand-me-downs or whatever, so getting to pick out brand new stuff for myself was a real luxury.

"I personally like the Hello Kitty one with the pink flowers." I looked up to see a tall blond guy leaning against the wall, watching me. He had a smirk on his face, and I wondered if he was making fun of me. He was definitely cute, but in a different way from the boy I'd seen earlier at Shadowford. That other guy,

Jackson, was very rebel-without-a-cause while this guy was all-American-pretty-boy.

I picked up the pink bag and held it out toward him, then closed one eye as if picturing him wearing it. "Yeah, I can see that. It brings out the natural rosiness of your cheeks."

He laughed and grabbed the bag from my hand, then placed it back on the rack. "Here," he said. "Most of the girls around here wear our school colors. Blue, like this one."

"What if I'm not like most other girls?"

"Ooh, a rebel. Nice," he said. A stray piece of hair fell across his forehead as he leaned down to get a different bag. His eyes were as blue as the summer sky. "What about black with blue stripes?"

"You're all about getting me to wear the school colors. What are you, some kind of backpack ambassador for the local team?"

His eyes sparkled when he laughed, sending a little jolt of energy through my body. What were the odds of me meeting two crush-worthy guys my age on my first day here? This town was looking better by the minute.

"Sort of," he said. "I'm the quarterback of the Demons football team."

Well, that certainly explained his muscular body and tall frame. I'd never dated a jock before, but suddenly, I wasn't so opposed to school pride. "Well, in that case, I'd better take your advice."

I chose a black bag with blue flowers embroidered on the outside and he placed his index finger on his lips and pretended to study it.

"It's a little girly, but I suppose it'll do." He smiled again, then held his hand out to me. "I'm Drake, by the way. Lori's my sister. Sometimes I come by and help her unload boxes on the weekends after church."

The touch of his hand on mine made me feel warm from head to toe. "Harper."

"You just moved here?" he asked.

"Yeah," I said. My face felt hot. Would he care that I lived at Shadowford? I was sure everyone in town knew what kind of place it was, and I wasn't expecting it to earn me any popularity points. It was only a matter of time before he found out, but I certainly didn't want to offer up bonus information. "From Atlanta."

"Cool," he said. "We don't get a lot of new people here. It'll be nice to get some new blood."

I was about to ask him more about the Demons football team when Agnes bumped into me, sending candles flying.

"Crap. Sorry Harper, I wasn't watching where-" Her voice cut out as she noticed Drake standing there. I bent down to help her pick up the candles she'd dropped.

"Do you two know each other?"

"Oh hey Drake," Agnes said, standing. Her pale skin was flushed pink and her breathing was uneven. "You did an awesome job at the game Friday night. I was there right up front cheering you on."

Drake's eyebrows came together slightly and he looked from me to Agnes, then back again. I knew that look. My heart fell.

"So you live at Shadowford?" he asked.

I tried to act like it was no big deal. I pulled my shoulders back. "Yeah. Just moved in today."

He looked around as if he were trying to find a way out of this situation. "I gotta run," he said, backing away. "Nice to meet you. Oh, and Agnes, make sure you pay for that stuff, especially if you broke any of those candles."

As Drake rushed off toward the back room, I stood there, feeling like the victim of a drive-by. What had just happened? Was he really that stuck-up? I'd experienced the cold-shoulder treatment in the past when people found out I was an orphan

BEAUTIFUL DEMONS

or a foster kid, but never anything quite as blatant as Drake's flirt-and-bolt.

"What was Drake talking to you about?" Agnes said.

I sighed and helped Agnes collect the rest of her candles and put them into my bag. "I don't know, backpacks, I guess."

"Isn't he gorgeous? He's the most popular senior boy in school. Good looking. Crazy rich. And even more important, completely single."

"He's also an asshole," I mumbled.

Agnes looked around. "Be quiet," she whispered. "You shouldn't say things like that in his sister's store. Besides, he's not like that at all."

"Were you paying attention at all just now? He was over here basically flirting with me, then when you walked over here and he realized I was from Shadowford, he turned into a grade-A jerk and got the hell away from us. In my book, that makes him a stuck-up asshole."

"I doubt he was flirting with you anyway," she said. "Guys like Drake only date cheerleaders."

"In movies, maybe."

Agnes looked at me curiously, as if I had no idea how the world really worked.

VOICES AT MY WINDOW

AFTER DINNER, I said goodnight and made my way up to my room. Agnes, for once, gave me a little bit of privacy. I shut the heavy wooden door to my room, but when I went to lock it, I noticed something strange. There were no locks on the inside of the door. The switch to lock the door was on the outside where you would expect to find a keyhole. I thought maybe mine had just been put on backwards, but when I looked over at the rooms of the other girls, I noticed theirs was exactly the same way. Locks on the outside.

I shut my door tight and wedged one of my flip-flops underneath. Maybe that was part of the Shadowford rule book. No privacy. I checked the bathroom and found no locks at all on that door. How could they expect me to take a shower or a bath in here without being able to lock my door? For now, the flipflop method would probably keep the door closed to intruders, but it wouldn't be enough to stop someone who was intent on getting in.

I considered making a "Do Not Enter" sign to let Agnes and the others know I wanted privacy, but I knew that if Ella Mae or Mrs. Shadowford wanted to come in, they could. Then again,

I thought, Mrs. Shadowford was in a wheelchair. I hadn't noticed any kind of elevator or special contraption to move her upstairs, so maybe it was only Ella Mae and the other girls I had to worry about when it came to privacy.

After I shoved another flip-flop under the bathroom door, I drew a warm bath and lowered myself into the refreshing bubbles. I guess I must have been pretty tired, because I fell asleep nearly the instant my body was immersed in the water.

I couldn't be sure how much time passed, but at some point, I started to dream. A woman in white floated down the hallway, her feet inches from the ground. She called out to me and I followed her. In my dream, we were here in Shadowford Manor. Somehow, I knew she was taking me to the third floor. As I walked down the dark corridor, I looked for the stairs, but there were none.

How do we get there? I asked her. There's no staircase.

She smiled and floated to the end of the hallway, beckoning me with a ghostly fingertip. The woman in white stopped in front of a section of the wall covered from floor to ceiling in wood paneling. She passed through it, and I tried to follow her, but couldn't. I could hear her calling to me from the other side of the wall. I placed my hands on the wooden panel, but when it wouldn't budge, I felt strangely powerless. I pounded against the wall, pushed with all my might, but the woman in white was gone.

I put my back to the wall and leaned against it. On the opposite wall was a large mirror. In it, I saw a bright red flash. Flames! Then, suddenly, a rush of heat came to me, as real as anything I'd ever felt. When I turned around to find the source of the fire, I was no longer at Shadowford. I had been transported back to my past, to a small two bedroom house I remembered all too well. I sat in the middle of my room, the remains of my angry tears still making a path down my cheeks as flames broke out around me. In the next room, I could hear a man screaming. Jill, with her porcelain doll skin and kind brown eyes, looked over at me.

"What have you done?" she asked. "You witch! Why did you do it?"

I tried to explain that I hadn't meant to start the fire. It was an accident. I reached out to her, but suddenly, the door burst open and water flooded in, filling the room in an instant. I floated up on the wave, then slowly sank to the bottom, unable to breathe.

I gasped and sat up in the bathtub in my room at Shadowford, splashing water and bubbles all over the tile floor. Leaning over the edge of the tub, I struggled for air.

The dream had been so vivid. The call of the woman's voice. The heat of the fire. I shivered, realizing the bathwater had long gone cold. I must have been asleep for a while. Carefully, I climbed out of the tub and wrapped myself in a towel.

In my room, it had grown dark since the sun went down. I switched on the bedside lamp and changed into my pajamas. Sleep threatened my eyes again, and I was asleep within minutes of sinking into my large canopied bed.

A scream woke me from my sleep. I bolted upright, my heart pounding.

The scream came again, blood-curdling this time. I heard real fear in the sound. I rushed to the door and yanked, but nothing happened. Then, remembering the flip-flop wedged in the bottom, I bent over and pulled it from the door. I tried to turn the knob, but it wouldn't move. Someone had locked me inside.

Panic seized my body. What if there was a fire? And I was locked inside? Had someone locked me in?

I banged against the door. "Help! Is anyone out there?"

I pressed my ear against the wood, expecting to hear more screams and chaos, but there was nothing. It was quiet.

"Hello?" I spoke through the door, but heard no answer. Surely someone was out there. Someone had locked me in. Someone had screamed bloody murder.

Now, it seemed, the house was quiet. I began to doubt my own ears. Maybe it had all been just another dream.

Then, voices at my window. The sound of breaking glass floated up to me and someone made a hushing sound. I tiptoed across the room and looked down. Even outside at midnight, the air was thick with heat. The motion sensor by the cottage out back had been triggered and the backyard was bathed in an eerie orange glow.

Down in the garden, movement caught my eye. I squinted to see who it was, but all I saw were shadows. Had someone outside been screaming? I didn't think so. I was certain the sound had come from inside the house, but whoever these people were outside, they didn't seem to have heard it.

"Be quiet." A guy's voice. He was somewhere in the darkness near the back of the garden, but I could almost make out his figure.

"Oh come on, Jackson." A giggle. A girl I didn't recognize. "Don't be such a stick in the mud."

"I'm serious, you can't be here," he said. "It's late. You should go home."

"Not until you give me what I want," the girl said. In the shadows, I saw her grab him and pull him close. His girlfriend?

But Jackson pushed the girl away. "Stop, Tori. You know that crap doesn't work on me."

"I don't understand you," she said. "What is it about you that's so different?"

Jackson emerged from the darkness and a blonde girl stumbled after him. "Wait! Aww, Jackson, come on." She grabbed his arm and he turned sharply toward her.

In the glow of the light from the barn, I could see the anger and frustration on his face. Inside, my heart pounded watching them. For a moment, I thought he might hit her, but instead, he yanked his arm away from her. "Just go."

The girl, Tori, had her back to me. She put her hands on her hips and backed away from him. "Fine. I didn't want anything from you anyway."

Jackson kicked at the grass as the girl walked around the side of the house. As if sensing me watching him, he looked up toward my room, just as he had done earlier that day. Quickly, I backed away from the window and closed the curtains.

In the distance, I heard a car start up and drive away.

THE BIG STONE
DEMON STATUE

"*N*ERVOUS?"

Agnes poked her head into my room Monday morning. I stifled a yawn and waved her in.

"More tired than anything," I said. "What was all that screaming about the past couple nights?"

Agnes cocked her head and made a face at me. "Screaming? What screaming?"

"You didn't hear it? I swear to God, it was like someone was getting slaughtered out there." I checked my outfit in the mirror. I was afraid I looked like I was trying too hard with my black lace skirt and black v-neck t-shirt. Maybe I looked too morbid. As an afterthought, I grabbed a plain pink ribbon and wrapped it around my wrist. "Tie this, would you?"

"Sure," Agnes said. "I slept like a baby last night. Sometimes Mary Anne has nightmares, but I've never heard her scream or anything. Maybe you dreamed it."

I thought about the locked door. "What freaked me out even more was the fact that I couldn't get out of my room to go see what was going on."

"What do you mean?"

"I mean, why are there locks on the outside of our doors. Why do they lock us in our rooms?"

Agnes shook her head, as if she didn't believe me. "I don't think they ever really lock them," she said.

But she was wrong. I knew!

"Stop worrying," Agnes said. "Besides, you look hot. That skirt is so cute. It's very punk."

I laughed. "Thanks."

"Grab your bag. You don't want to be late for your first day."

Together, we made our way down to the Shadowford van. I had half hoped we'd be taking the bus to school, but no such luck. They might as well have mounted a megaphone on top and shouted to everyone that we were freaks. I sighed. After the way Drake had treated me, I fully expected everyone at school to label me an outcast right away.

In the van, Mary Anne and Courtney barely said a word. I wondered what things must have been like before I came along. Did Agnes talk their ears off nonstop? Or was she only this talkative because she hadn't had anyone else to talk to in so long?

"I'll show you where to go to get your class schedule," Agnes said as we pulled up to the high school ten minutes later. "We're both sophomores, so hopefully we'll have a few classes together."

I stepped out onto the concrete sidewalk and stared at the school. My stomach lurched. God, I hated starting new schools. With this latest string of foster homes, I'd started four different schools in the past two years. Peachville High School made five.

The school itself was even smaller than I expected. A single brick building held most of the classes with only the gymnasium and one other small building off near the football field. Most of the schools I'd been to in Atlanta had more students in the tenth grade than this school probably had all combined. I tried to tell myself it would be an adventure. A kind of social experiment. Inside, though, I just felt nervous.

In big schools, you could always find your own crowd. There were always enough people around that you were bound to run into a few people who thought like you, looked like you, or at least were interested in getting to know you. Here, though, I had a feeling the variety was limited. Looking around at the students as they made their way to the front entrance, I noticed that almost everyone dressed the same. Jeans. T-shirts. Blue and black backpacks. Very apple-pie American teenager. Suddenly I felt silly with my black skirt and boots. I gripped my new bag tighter and silently thanked Drake Ashworth for giving me at least one solid tip on how to fit in.

If I was going to make it work here in Peachville, I was going to have to find a way to blend.

"If you stand there long enough, you're going to turn into a statue like this guy." Agnes smacked the leg of the big stone demon statue that towered over the school's entrance.

I stared up at the demon, and for a moment, I felt all the breath leave my chest. I could swear I had seen that statue somewhere before. In a dream maybe? The ground seemed to jerk underneath my feet and I stumbled, reaching out to the cold stone to steady myself. My vision blurred, then the world around me turned black.

I MUST BE
ELECTRO-CHARGED

*I*N THE DISTANCE, I heard Agnes calling my name.

Slowly, my eyes opened to find a crowd standing around me.

"Give her some room students." A beautiful woman with dark black hair stood over me, her face full of concern. "What's your name?"

I opened my mouth and sucked in a huge breath. "Harper," I said. The sun was bright and I squinted against it. "What happened?"

"I'm Mrs. King," the woman said. "You fainted, but I think you're going to be okay. Do you think you can sit up?"

I nodded, mortified. And, oh, God, I was wearing a skirt. I pulled down on the lace, hoping I hadn't flashed anyone on my way down.

"How are you feeling?" Mrs. King asked.

"Embarrassed," I said, trying to laugh it off. The crowd around me began to disperse, and I was grateful. In a town this small, though, I knew it wouldn't take long for word to get around that the latest Shadowford freak fainted on her first day of school.

Agnes took my hand and helped me to my feet. "I can't believe that just happened. I mean, I was standing there talking to you one second, and the next you were down. Bam! Just like that." She slapped her hands together. "Thank goodness Mrs. King was walking up."

"Thank you," I said. "I think I'm going to be fine."

Mrs. King smiled and took my hand. I felt a shock of static electricity and pulled away. I laughed it off, but Mrs. King eyed me suspiciously. The serious look on her face startled me, and I wondered if I had done something wrong.

"Sorry," I mumbled, thinking about how the doorknob in Mrs. Shadowford's office had shocked me the other day too. "That's been happening to me a lot lately. I must be electro-charged or something."

"It's fine," Mrs. King said. She took my hand again and helped me up. "Let me walk you to the office and make sure you get checked in okay."

I tried to take my hand back, but something had caught her eye. She stared at my chin with a seriousness that sent a cold shiver down my spine. "Is everything okay?"

"Yes," she said absently. "That's a beautiful necklace." She let go of my hand and reached out to touch the sapphire pendant around my neck. "Where did you get it?"

"It was my mother's." On instinct, I grasped the pendant between my thumb and forefinger and ran it back and forth across the silver chain. The necklace was the only thing I had ever known of my real mother.

Mrs. King stared at me for a moment, then she shook her head and smiled again. "Well, then, let's get you to the office, shall we?"

"Wow, she was super nice to you," Agnes said once Mrs. King had left us by the entrance to the office. We watched as a sea of students parted to let her pass.

"Is she not usually nice?"

"No, it's not that, it's just that she's kind of hard to get close to. She heads up the cheerleaders and they're just so exclusive. I've been trying to get on the squad for the past two years."

"You make it sound like the cheerleaders are some kind of goddesses around here," I said, pushing my way into the office.

Agnes mumbled something under her breath that I didn't quite catch.

"What?" I asked her.

"Nothing." Her attitude changed, like I had offended her or something. "I gotta get to class. Hope you're feeling better."

I shook my head and sighed. Was no one in this town normal?

SOMEONE MIGHT GET HURT

*E*XCEPT FOR THE whole passing out in front of everyone thing, my morning went by without further incident. Classes here were small, but I was relieved to find that most of them were far behind where we were in my Atlanta school. At least I wouldn't have to worry about being behind on homework, especially since Ella Mae had been so serious about me keeping my grades up.

At lunch, I found Agnes and walked over to her, hoping she had gotten over whatever I'd done to make her mad this morning. She was sitting with three other girls who looked up as I walked over.

"Hey," I said. "Mind if I sit with y'all?"

"Sure," she said, her bubbly attitude thankfully returned. "This is Harper everyone. Harper, this is Shamekia, Randi, and Flora."

"Hey," Randi said. "How's your day going so far?"

"Hi," I said, sitting down. "Typical school day, I guess. How about y'all?"

"Always the same," Agnes said. "Too bad we don't have any classes together. I have math after lunch. What's next for you?" She squirted some ketchup onto her plate and dipped a french fry into it.

I glanced at my schedule, then slipped it back into my bag. "Sixth period Calculus," I said.

Agnes coughed, nearly spitting out her fry. "I thought you said you were a sophomore?"

"I am."

"Then how are you in calculus? That's usually a senior class."

I shrugged. "I don't know. I'm not even sure they have my transcripts here yet. Maybe they put me in the wrong thing."

Agnes brightened. "Yeah, that's probably it. I mean, sophomores are hardly ever in the same class with seniors. I bet once they get your transcripts, they'll move you into my class."

"Uh-huh," I said, stuffing a french fry into my mouth. I didn't want to tell her that I had been taking calculus at my last school too. She seemed sensitive when it came to certain things, and I didn't want to make her angry again or hurt her feelings. I figured it was best to feign ignorance. And change the subject. "So what's there to do around here for fun? Like on the weekends?"

Agnes didn't answer me. In fact, I don't even think she heard me. Her hand was stuck mid-way to her mouth and her eyes were glued to something on the opposite side of the cafeteria. I turned and followed her gaze.

That's when I saw them. A group of four girls more beautiful than anyone had a right to be. They seemed to glide across the room as a single unit. Nearly everyone in the cafeteria was staring at them. As they passed, a younger boy with glasses practically tripped over himself to get out of their way.

"Who are they?" I asked.

"Those are the cheerleaders," Agnes said.

Her tone carried a certain reverence, and I had to hold back a laugh. Man, these people really seemed to take their sports seriously. There was definitely something special about those girls, but other than their beauty, I wasn't sure why everyone was so awed by them.

"There are only four cheerleaders?"

Agnes looked at me and rolled her eyes. "No, silly. Those are just the four most popular cheerleaders. The girl on the right, the brunette? She's Brooke Harris, senior and captain of the squad."

I turned to look at the girl she was talking about. She had shoulder-length brown hair and was wearing tight black pants and a beaded pink tank top. Her smile lit up her entire face. "Lark Chen is the Asian girl next to Brooke," Shamekia said, nodding toward the cheerleaders. "Her mom is the mayor."

Lark was shorter than the others. Her bone-straight hair fell halfway down her back and was the color of obsidian. She was talking excitedly to the girl next to her.

"Then there's Allison Moore. She's got the most beautiful blue eyes. And don't you guys love her hair now that she's leaving it curly?" Flora said.

"Allison used to date Drake Ashworth," Agnes said, poking me in the ribs. I turned to study the girl with the dark blonde ringlets. She was cute and petite. Exactly the kind of girl who would look great with a guy like Drake.

"And the girl on the end. The unreal blond with the big smile? Thats-"

"Tori," I said, interrupting Shamekia.

"Yeah," she said. "Do you know her?"

"Not exactly," I said. But I had seen her before. My first night at Shadowford, she was the girl arguing with Jackson by the garden. She seemed so different this morning. Not at all like the kind of girl who needed to throw herself at a guy to get what she wanted. I wondered what exactly it was she wanted from Jackson anyway.

Agnes eyed me suspiciously. "Seriously, how did you know her name?"

"I think I might have a class with her," I lied.

"Yeah, that would make sense," Flora said. "Tori and Allison are in our grade, but Lark is a junior and Brooke is a senior. They're all best friends."

"I would give anything to sit over there with them at lunch, even just once," Randi said.

"I know, they are seriously the most beautiful girls in school," Agnes said.

I looked around and realized that since the four cheerleaders had stepped into the room, they had commanded the attention of nearly every table. It was weird. Sure, they were beautiful, but the way people were falling all over themselves to be noticed by them gave them almost celebrity-level status. As soon as they sat down at their table in the center of the lunchroom, a group of younger girls came over with cold bottles of water, as if they were servants. I didn't get it.

Of course, I was staring just like everyone else. I watched as the cheerleaders were soon joined by several other people, one of which caught my eye. Drake Ashworth. I tried not to stare at him, especially after the way he treated me at his sister's store, but there was a part of me that was curious about him. At first, he'd seemed so nice and sweet, but then he'd changed in a heartbeat.

"You can quit staring," Agnes whispered. "Guys like Drake-"

"I know," I said. "They only date cheerleaders."

"Exactly," she said. "He's definitely gorgeous, but he's just out of our league, trust me."

She was probably right, but the way he'd flirted with me before he knew I was from Shadowford. Well, he genuinely seemed interested.

When I went to dump my lunch tray, I walked by his table, just to see if he would notice me and maybe say hi. Unfortunately, I was too busy watching him instead of watching my feet, and I accidentally tripped over someone's backpack. My tray went flying, sending ketchup and left-over french fries flying.

I watched in horror as ketchup splattered all over Tori's white shirt.

"Jesus, what the hell?" She stood up and threw her hands into the air with disgust. Then, she looked up at me.

My face burned with fresh embarrassment. Of all people to fling ketchup on...why, God, why? It just wasn't my day.

"Sorry," I said. "I must have tripped on something." I looked back to see what I might have stumbled over, but the floor was clear. I could have sworn I felt my boot hit something solid, but there was nothing there now.

"You've got to be kidding me," she yelled. "You are so dead. Who the hell are you anyway? I've never seen you here before."

"Oh, Tori, didn't you hear about the latest resident of Shadowford's home for rejects?" Lark said with a laugh. "She fainted right in front of the school this morning."

"That's right," Brooke added. "I heard they were getting a new freak over there. They should have warned us that she was so clumsy."

"What happened? Did you get too nervous on your first day of school little girl?" Allison said.

Everyone around the table laughed, and I looked to Drake, hoping to find at least one friendly face. He met my eye for an instant, then looked away. Coward.

I straightened my shoulders, bracing myself against the painful blow to my ego. "Sorry about your shirt," I said. "It really was an accident."

"Oh, you'll be sorry alright. What was your name again?"
"Harper."
"Well, Harper, you just made the wrong kind of enemy."

The look in Tori's eyes was stormy and wild. My heart beat raced in my chest. I needed to get out of there. I moved to step around her and retrieve my tray, but she stepped with me and blocked my path.

"Look, I said I was sorry. What more can I do?"

I stepped to the other side, but she blocked me again. I felt the heat of anger and humiliation boil up inside of me. My fingers tingled with a familiar buzz, and I took in a deep breath. I couldn't lose control. Not here. Not on my first day.

Someone might get hurt.

On the table, my lunch tray rattled, then rose slightly into the air. I gasped and the tray fell to the table with a loud smack. Everyone around me grew silent.

Across the table, Drake's eyes met mine, wide and scared.

"I told you she was a freak," Brooke said, breaking the silence. Some of her confidence was gone, though, as if I had surprised her. "Come on, y'all. Let's get out of here before she really goes mental."

I stood there as the group of popular kids filed past me.

Tori stopped inches from my face and narrowed her eyes at me. "Cross me again and I'll make you pay," she said.

I had officially made my first enemy at Peachville High School.

WHAT IS IT WITH THIS TOWN AND CHEERLEADERS?

I LET OUT A frustrated gurgle and kicked the brick as hard as I could with my boot. Never in a million years did I dream my first day could go this badly. I wanted to go home, and it wasn't even noon yet.

"Hit those bricks any harder and you just might bring the whole building down."

I twirled around to see who was talking. I sucked in a tight breath when I saw Jackson Hunt standing there at the edge of the building, cigarette in hand and a ridiculously sexy smile on his face. He was even better looking up close than I thought he'd be.

"I'm serious," he said. "You've got some kind of kick there. I'm impressed."

I laughed, then groaned. "This is positively the worst first day of school ever."

"And just think, it's not over yet."

"Thanks, that gives me something to look forward to," I said.

He smiled. "I'm Jackson."

"I know," I said, then felt like smacking myself for admitting it. "I saw you from my window the other day. I'm Harper."

"So, Harper, where did you learn to move objects with your mind?"

My eyes widened in surprise. No one had ever called me out like that before. I didn't know how to respond. "If you're just here to make fun of me, I think I've had enough for one day if you don't mind," I said, suddenly feeling very defensive. I waited for him to call me a witch or tell me I was some kind of freak.

"Whoa, that's not what I mean. I think it's pretty neat what you did in there. Seriously."

I turned to study his face. He seemed to be telling the truth. "You don't think I'm a complete nut-case?"

"No," he said. "Trust me. Stranger things have happened."

I leaned against the jagged bricks and sighed. Right. Stranger things than floating lunch trays? I doubted it.

"Don't worry about it so much," Jackson said. "It was kind of funny, really."

"No, it was completely stupid. Everyone seems to worship those girls, so what do I do? Make them my enemies? Real smart."

"Well, you made me laugh," he said. He moved beside me and leaned one hand against the brick. "Plus, you have no idea how nice it was to see someone dump ketchup all over the precious Tori Fairchild."

I wondered again what his relationship to her was. It was obvious they didn't run in the same circles here at school, and yet she had practically been all over him the other night.

"I hope it was worth it. Because now she wants me dead."

Jackson lowered his voice and leaned so close I could smell his shampoo. "Something tells me you can hold your own against those girls."

My palms began to sweat, and I felt suddenly short of breath at the nearness of him.

"Can I ask you a question?"

He raised his eyebrows. "Shoot."

"Why does everyone worship them? I mean, they're beautiful, but..." I shrugged. "Lots of people in this world are beautiful."

"They're popular because they're cheerleaders," he said.

I rolled my eyes. "What is it with this town and cheerleaders? Jesus."

Jackson laughed, making his green eyes come alive. My heart sort of melted a bit watching him. Then, he shook his head and squashed his cigarette into the ground.

"They're poisonous, Harper. They get into your system and change you from the inside." His expression smoothed over suddenly, like it was too much for him to explain. He pushed off the wall. "Don't let them get to you."

His words fell heavy on my ears as I watched him walk away.

MY BEST ATTEMPT

"*Y*OU HAVE TO wear blue and black." Agnes poked her head into my room and made a face at me in the mirror. "Demon pride!"

She was wearing a demon tattoo on her face like all the cheerleaders at school. She held one out to me and asked if I wanted help putting it on, but I stuck my tongue out at her. There was no way I was going to wear a blue demon on my face.

"Fine," she said. "You don't have to wear the demon, but you can at least put on a blue t-shirt."

I bit my lip and stared into my sparsely populated closet. Besides the pink tee I was currently wearing, I had a total of twelve shirts. None of them were blue. "How about black?"

She shrugged. "I guess that'll work."

"Why do we have to go to this stupid game anyway?"

"It's tradition," she said. "It's like a family outing during football season. Mrs. Shadowford never goes for obvious reasons, but Ella Mae likes the games. I think she used to be a cheerleader when she was in school."

I rolled my eyes. Cheerleaders. It was like I couldn't get away from them in this town.

"I'm going to try out for the cheerleading squad next year again," she said. She fell backward onto my bed and sighed. "I'm already nervous about it and tryouts aren't even until June."

"Why would you want to be a cheerleader?" I asked, thinking about how mean Tori and her friends were.

"Who wouldn't want to be part of that crowd?" she said. "They're the most beautiful girls in school." Agnes stood up and started leafing through my notebook of drawings that lay open on the end of the bed.

"Yeah, but just because you become a cheerleader doesn't mean you'll suddenly become beautiful," I said.

"Ouch. That was totally mean."

I spun around, black tank top in hand. "Oh, Agnes, I didn't mean it like that. You're adorable."

She sighed. "I know I'm not ugly or anything, but you just don't understand. When a girl makes the squad, she... changes."

"How?"

"You wouldn't understand," Agnes said. "It's like a makeover in a way. Take Allison, for example. A few years ago, she was kind of an ugly duckling. Then, she made it onto the cheerleading squad at the end of her eighth grade year. When we came back as freshman, it was like she was totally transformed. Like some kind of summer miracle."

I changed into the black tank and searched through my stash of colorful ribbons for something demon blue. I found a royal blue silk ribbon and handed it to Agnes. She tied it around my wrist.

"What's up with all the ribbons?" she asked.

"One of my foster moms worked at a crafts store. She always used to bring home tons of leftover ribbons," I said, feeling lame. "I don't know, I just like to wear them for color."

"Do you have another blue one?" she asked.

I smiled. "Sure," I said, and helped her fasten a matching blue ribbon around her ponytail.

"These are really good you know." She pointed to the drawings in my notebook. "Are you going to be an artist or something?"

"Probably not. I kind of suck." The truth was that I yearned to take art classes. Unfortunately, most of the public schools I'd been to had really crappy art programs, and there was no way I could afford to take classes anywhere else. I didn't like to talk about my art too much though. In my experience, sharing too much about your dreams and goals with someone was pretty much just giving them fuel to hurt you later. "It's really just for fun anyway."

"Okay, girls," Ella Mae called from downstairs. "I've got the van out front. You've got five minutes to get downstairs!"

Agnes took off running, but I hung back to see which picture she had been staring at with such intensity. The book was open to a pencil drawing I'd done of my mother. She gave me up for adoption when I was born, but I found a picture of her in my adopted parents' files once. They took it away from me and hid it somewhere, but I spent weeks after that trying to recreate it with my pencils. The drawing Agnes had been staring at was my best attempt.

"Harper," Ella Mae called. "Everybody's waiting for you, honey. Let's go."

I ran my finger across the drawing of the pendant my mother wore around her neck, then closed the notebook with a snap.

"Coming," I yelled, then headed down the stairs to join the group.

MAYBE HE WASN'T A DEMONS FAN

RIDAY NIGHT FOOTBALL at the Peachville High stadium was like going to a fair without all the rides. There was popcorn, cotton candy, music, and practically everyone in town came. Ella Mae gave us each money for admission and snacks, then told us to meet her back at the Shadowford van ten minutes after the final buzzer.

Mary Anne, who had yet to say two words to me since I moved to Peachville, took off to sit with Ella Mae. Courtney, Agnes and I stuck together.

"So, what do you want to do?" Agnes said. "We could find a spot on the bleachers and watch the kickoff. Or we could get something to eat. We could always walk around and look for cute guys. There's this one guy, Grant, that's in my English class. He's delicious. I'll introduce you to him if I see him. I have a major crush on him."

We walked along the back of the metal bleachers. Agnes talked nonstop and I tried to pretend I wasn't searching for

Jackson in the crowd. He hadn't been with us on the Shadowford van, but his car wasn't in the driveway either.

"What about you?" she asked.

"What?"

"You know, boys. Did you have a boyfriend in Atlanta?"

I shook my head. "Not really. There was this one guy, Lucas. He was sort of my boyfriend for a while, but I've moved around too much to stay with anyone."

"I know what you mean," Agnes said. "Before Shadowford, I had been in like eight different schools."

"What about you, Courtney?" I wanted to include her in the conversation, but for the most part, Courtney seemed really shy.

"I've never had a boyfriend," she said.

"Is there anyone at PHS that you like?" Agnes asked. "You've been going to school here for what? Four years now?"

"Uh-huh." Courtney pushed her straight blond hair out of her face, and for the first time, I noticed how pretty she was. "There's no one really special, I guess."

"I think we should try to find a boyfriend for Harper."

"Whoa, no thanks," I said, shaking my head vigorously. It wasn't that I was opposed to having a boyfriend, of course, I just didn't want Agnes picking him out for me. My mind flashed to Jackson's dark green eyes and the way my entire body had gone hot when he came close to me.

"We'll see," she said with a smile. "It won't be hard for a girl like you."

"Why do you say that?"

"Just look at you," Agnes said. "You're tall, skinny. You have perfect skin. And I'd kill to have such pretty wavy blonde hair. You know, you're pretty enough-"

"If you tell me I'm pretty enough to be a cheerleader, I'm gonna punch you in the face," I joked.

She giggled and bumped me jokingly with her shoulder. "Fine, I won't say it."

As we turned the corner, I scanned the parking lot again for Jackson's car, but there was no sign of him. Maybe he wasn't a demon fan.

The announcer's voice boomed through the loudspeaker. "Welcome Demon fans to another night of Peachville High football!"

"Come on," Agnes said, taking my hand. "Let's go down to the field to watch the team break through the banner."

As we made our way down to the field, I watched as the cheerleaders unfolded a huge banner that said "GO DEMONS! BEAT THE HOGS!" in bright blue letters. The marching band stood in two lines blaring pep music while the fans crowded onto the field, forming a sort of runway for the team.

Toward the front, I could see Tori Fairchild standing on another cheerleader's shoulders. She was admittedly gorgeous, and from here she actually looked human. It sucked that after only one week at school, there was already someone who made my stomach hurt when I saw them. Especially when it was one of the town's golden girls.

Just then, the band started up the school's fight song and the team broke through the banner, bursting onto the field amid roars from the crowd. I clapped along without enthusiasm. Boys in blue and black shiny football jerseys rushed by, some of them jumping into the air to rile up the fans. Drake Ashworth passed in front of me, and I felt a stab of hurt.

He'd been so nice to me when we first met. Flirty, even. But all week at school, he'd treated me like I was a nobody. A social outcast. Not once had he acknowledged our conversation in his sister's store or the fact that he even knew who I was. To make matters worse, he was in my calculus class, the one disadvantage to being put in a senior level course. Once, I'd caught him staring at me during class, but when I smiled, he'd gotten a distasteful look on his face, then turned away.

"He's so cute, isn't he?" Agnes said, forcing me to look away.

"Who?"

"Drake. That is who you're staring at right? And don't say no. I've seen the way you stare at him sometimes in the caf."

I followed the crowd back toward the bleachers. "I have no idea what you're talking about."

"Okay, say what you will, but I know the truth, don't I Courtney?"

Courtney shrugged and looked at me with an apology in her eyes. Her hair hung over her face again and her shoulders hunched slightly forward. No doubt she had been putting up with Agnes' match-making for a couple of years now. I winked at her to show her that I wasn't bothered by it, and she smiled shyly back at me.

"Let's find a seat on the bleachers," I said.

I wasn't surprised when Agnes picked a spot a few rows in front of the cheerleaders. She argued that she needed to watch their cheers closely so she could practice them at home. I for one didn't understand why she was already thinking about tryouts that were still a good eight or nine months away, but I wasn't going to force her to sit somewhere else.

Brooke, the dark-haired senior captain, started most of the cheers, and I was amazed at how actively the crowd participated. Sure, most schools had a section that would cheer along with the group cheers. But this crowd? They were obsessed. When Brooke started cheering "Give me a D!", the entire home side of the stadium roared back, "D!". It was honestly so loud, it startled me. Talk about team spirit. As the game went on, I started to wonder if more people had come to watch the cheerleaders than the actual football game, which, by the way, the Demons won, 34-10. Much to my dismay, Drake Ashworth was a talented quarterback. There had been a small part of me that hoped he would suck so I could boo him when his passes were intercepted. No such luck.

"Great game," Agnes said on the way back to the Shadowford van.

"Thrilling," I said.

"You're going to have to learn some school spirit if you plan to come to the games with me from now on," she said, teasing. "I have a feeling the Demons will grow on you once you've been here for a while. We've got a great team this year."

Considering the fact that all of the cheerleaders had it out for me and the team's quarterback had treated me like roadkill, I seriously doubted I'd be donning a Demon tattoo and buying blue pompoms anytime soon. The game's one redeeming moment happened as we walked into the parking lot. I heard laughter erupt somewhere off to my right, and when I looked to find the source, I saw Jackson Hunt sitting on the hood of a car with a few guys I didn't recognize.

Before I could stop myself, I smiled and waved. Jackson, who had been heckling some poor Demons fan who was decked out in full blue face paint, looked my way. His normally spiky dark hair fell forward over his face slightly, framing his dark eyes. A wave of warmth washed over me as our eyes met.

He lifted his eyebrows suggestively, then the corners of his mouth lifted slightly in a smile that made his mouth look oh-so-kissable. I melted from head to toe in a rush of desire. Never in my life had a guy inspired such a raw physical reaction in my body. I felt drawn to him.

Did he feel it too?

"Who are you staring at?" Agnes asked, standing on her tippy-toes to see around the crowd.

Courtney glanced over at me and smiled, then hung her head forward. So she had seen my blush. She knew my secret crush. I wondered if she would betray it to Agnes, but she climbed into the van without a word, leaving Agnes to wonder what she'd missed.

"No one," I said.

"You saw someone," she said, climbing in after Courtney. "Trust me, I know that look. Harper likes a boy."

I laughed and glanced back over toward Jackson's car, but he was turned away, talking to his friends. Out of habit, I reached up to touch my mother's sapphire pendant. It was a movement I made a hundred times a day without even thinking about it. Only this time, the pendant was gone.

THAT NECKLACE WAS EVERYTHING TO ME

"*I* HAVE TO GO back," I said, tears already stinging the corners of my eyes.

"No Ma'am," Ella Mae said. "We need to get going or we'll be waiting in this lot forever."

"I dropped something important. I can't leave without it."

My eyes pleaded with Ella Mae and she took pity on me. "Be quick, alright?"

I ran back to the stadium, going over every step we'd taken throughout the night. The bleachers. The field. The concession stand. My necklace wasn't anywhere. I needed more time.

"Dammit," I said. I kicked the wooden light post hard. A sharp pain ran through my big toe and tears rolled down my cheeks. That necklace was too important. I couldn't lose it now, after all these years.

"What did you lose?" Agnes asked, coming around the corner to join me.

"My mother's necklace." I wiped my cheeks with the back of my hand and sniffed. I was acting like a baby, but that necklace was everything to me.

"Oh no, Harper. I'm so sorry. Was it expensive?"

"No, it's not like that. It's not about money. That pendant was the only thing of my mother's I'd ever owned. I never knew my mother," I said. "She gave me up for adoption when I was a baby. My parents gave me that necklace the day they told me I was adopted. They said my mother wanted me to have it. It's completely irreplaceable."

Agnes touched my arm. I saw genuine sympathy in her eyes. "That sucks," she said. "I'm sorry but Ella Mae asked me to come get you. I don't think she's going to wait much longer."

I knew I couldn't afford to make Ella Mae angry. One bad report to my case manager could land me in kid-prison if I wasn't careful.

"Maybe you can come back and look for it on Monday," she said.

I swiped at my tears again, then followed Agnes back to the van.

"Did you find it?" Ella Mae asked.

I shook my head and climbed into the van. I didn't say another word the entire way home.

LATER, ONCE EVERYONE was in bed, I tried to fall asleep. I really did, but there was no use. I couldn't stand the thought of someone else picking up that sapphire pendant, and I definitely couldn't stand the idea of it sitting there in the dirt with people's gum wrappers and coke cans. What if someone stepped on the stone and broke it?

I tossed and turned, unable to let it go. I only had this one piece of my mother. It was the only thing important enough for her to want me to have it. I needed to get it back.

Quietly, I got out of bed and tiptoed to my door. I slowly turned the brass handle, but as I suspected, the door was locked. I cursed through gritted teeth. Agnes was wrong about the doors. Why were they locking us in our rooms at night? And it wasn't every night. Only sometimes. I'd checked. Were they afraid we would have secret meetings or sneak out to meet boys?

Granted, sneaking out was exactly what I was trying to do, but a simple locked door wasn't about to stop me. I looked around for something I could use to turn the lock inside the keyhole. On my dressing table, I had a bag of bobby pins. I took one out, straightened it, and pulled off the little rubber tip.

Crouching down, I inserted the bobby pin into the hole, going by feel until I was able to slowly turn the lock mechanism inside the door. It only took me a few minutes of trying until I heard the distinct click that released the lock.

The dark hallway outside my bedroom door was silent as a tomb. The gentle whoosh of air conditioning was the only sound. I stepped lightly down onto the top step and winced as it creaked beneath my sneakers. Frozen, I didn't make a single move until I was sure no one had heard me.

Slowly, I made my way down the stairs and out the front door.

Once outside, I searched for a way to get into town. Starting up the Shadowford van would be way too loud. Plus, someone might see me. It was just too risky. What I needed was a bicycle. And there was only one place I could think to look.

The barn.

I made my way to the back of the house, mindful of every noise that rose above the steady song of crickets in the Georgia night. The motion sensor light above the barn door clicked on as I approached, and I hurried through the lit circle.

The door was tough to open, but I finally managed to crack it enough to squeeze inside. I couldn't see much beyond a huge spider web right in the entrance, but it was clear the building was bigger than I first realized. A couple of cars by the far wall were covered up with off-white tarps. A pegboard wall held carefully organized tools. Hammers, wrenches, a hand axe. Then, against the wall near the back, I saw the silhouette of a bicycle.

TORI HAS A SECRET

THE RIDE INTO town took nearly half an hour. The air seemed to grow cooler and as I rode, goosebumps jumped out on my arms and legs. High in the night sky, a half-moon rose up, giving a little needed light along the deserted road. Never in my life had I seen so many stars.

In the city, the stars were hard to see unless it was a super clear night. But out here in the middle of nowhere, the universe opened up to me. I felt small and insignificant as I rode those few miles watching the star-scattered night. And at the same time, I felt free, confident that once I made it to the stadium, I would find my mother's necklace.

The parking lot of the school was deserted. I rode up as close to the fence as I could get and looked for a way in, but all of the gates were locked up. The chain links were small enough for me to fit the tip of my shoe into and hoist myself over. I climbed up the fence, threw my leg over the top, then jumped down onto the dirt below.

From the looks of it, the janitor had already done a sweep of the stadium. Most of the popcorn boxes, drink cups, and trash were taken away, leaving only the plain dirt and sparse grass. I prayed the necklace was still there somewhere, or at the very least, picked up by someone and turned into lost and found where I could get it on Monday. I retraced every one of my steps from the second I had entered the gate until the time I left.

I walked from one side of the stadium to the other, looked through the metal bleachers, and searched around in the dirt. The pendant and chain were nowhere to be found. The longer I searched, the more frustrated I became.

My last ditch effort was to crawl beneath the bleachers and search for it there in the dirt and filth below where Agnes and I sat to watch the game. I walked down to the approximate place, then got on my hands and knees in the dirt to crawl beneath the seats. It was dark out there, but the stadium's emergency lights were still on. I ran my palm against the dirt and grass, pulling up every piece of trash or debris to inspect, just in case.

That's when I heard someone giggling. I recognized her right away. After all, Tori Fairchild was one of the first people I'd met at Peachville High, and I'd heard enough of her to last me a lifetime. Geez, it was like she was following me around like a little black raincloud. I froze in place, hoping she wouldn't see me there covered in dirt.

She skipped across the field, still in her blue and black Demons cheerleading uniform. There was a guy with her. In the semi-darkness, I couldn't quite make him out, but there was no doubt in my mind who it was. Who else would she be out here with after the game? He was wearing a Demons letterman jacket with a blue Demon on the back and a Demons baseball cap.

Foster Adams. Star receiver. They were the perfect couple.

I'd seen them together at school all week. Foster was one of the rich kids in town. He drove a freaking Porsche, if you get my drift. He was part of that elite crowd. You know, the one that hated me?

Tori rushed into his arms and he spun her around. Her high pitched giggles echoed off the bleachers and into the empty stadium. They both seemed so normal. So all-American high school kids. Would I ever have a normal life like that?

My legs started to cramp, but I didn't want them to see me crawling out from under the bleachers. I'd never hear the end of it. Plus, if anyone at Shadowford found out I was here, I'd be kicked out on my ass. I couldn't let that happen, so I crouched through the pain.

Tori and Foster stopped and embraced in a long, passionate kiss. I rolled my eyes and looked away. As I turned my head, I lost my balance. I let out a whoop as I fell backwards, hitting my head on one of the metal steps.

I drew in a nervous breath, my heart pounding like a jackhammer. My head snapped around to see if the others had heard me, and I was mortified to see them looking my way.

Oh God, I'll never hear the end of this.

The guy took a couple of steps in my direction.

"Who's there?" It didn't sound like Foster's voice, but then again, I hadn't heard him speak that many times. Tonight, though, his voice sounded deeper. Older.

I bit my lip, not daring to move an inch.

Tori leaned over to the guy and said something, but I couldn't quite make it out. She was pulling furiously on his arm, as if she were scared. Not that I could blame her. For all she knew, some maniac with a gun was out here to spy on them or rob them blind.

"Let's get out of here," Tori said.

"I wanna know who's there," the guy said. His face was still cloaked in shadow, but as he moved closer, I was certain it wasn't Foster. He was a bit too tall and not quite as muscular.

Tori has a secret, I thought. *Powerful information to have if I ever need it.*

I strained my eyes to make out the guy's face, but with the cap pulled firmly over his forehead, I simply couldn't tell who it was.

"There," Tori said, pointing toward the bleachers where I was hiding. "Under the bleachers."

The man came running toward me and out of fear, I bolted, slipping on the loose dirt a few times before I found my footing. I ran as fast as I could to the fence, scrambled over the top, and rode away. Just as I reached the edge of the parking lot, I could see the guy come around the side of the bleachers, too late to see my face.

FOR A GIRL LIKE YOU

B Y THE TIME I pulled down the driveway twenty minutes later, I was exhausted. I had no idea if Tori and her guy were going to jump in their car and follow me, so I pushed my body to the limit. My lungs burned. Cold tears spilled down my cheeks from the wind in my face. My legs were sore. But I pushed on.

I barely had the energy to pull open the large, stiff wooden door. Inside the barn, I stopped to catch my breath and noticed the pungent smell of cigarette smoke. Suddenly alert, I looked to either side, then saw the red burning end of Jackson Hunt's cigarette.

"Smoking will kill you, you know," I said, certain he'd been watching me.

"So will sneaking out at night." He stood and moved close enough that I could make out his face in the shadows. "Or so I've heard."

"Is this what you do in here, all secret like?"

"This," he said, "and work on my motorcycle." He motioned toward the back of the barn, but I couldn't see much of anything that far back.

"Do you ride?"

"I used to. It's my dad's old bike. A good one too. A Harley."

"Did your parents split? Or what?" I leaned against the wooden wall of the barn and ran my fingers along the smooth wood. Being this close to Jackson, especially in the dark, made me nervous.

"My dad passed away when I was a little boy." He didn't elaborate, and I didn't push. "Want a smoke?"

"No way," I said, sticking out my tongue and screwing up my nose. "It's completely disgusting."

He laughed and threw his cigarette to the ground. "For a girl like you, I might consider quitting."

The tone of his voice turned my body to melted chocolate. I steadied myself against the wall, afraid that if he moved any closer, I really would melt. I felt his nearness in my bones, a vibration of warm, flushed energy.

"You better get inside," he said, checking his watch even though it was probably too dark to see the time. The way he raised his arm and leaned forward brought his chest so close to me, I wanted to run my hand along the rippled muscles I felt certain I would find underneath his black t-shirt. "It's way past your bedtime."

My heart beat so hard in my chest my ears were filled with the loud thumping sound of it. I dipped under his arm and pushed open the barn door, grateful for the refreshing rush of cool, night air.

"I won't tell if you won't," I said.

"Your secret's safe with me," Jackson said. He drew an X over his heart as I ran toward the house, disappearing into the shadows.

WHAT WITH TORI'S DISAPPEARANCE

THE REST OF the weekend passed by in a daze. I couldn't stop thinking about Jackson. Plus, I was anxious to know if anyone had found my necklace. I didn't get much sleep.

On Monday morning at school, the first place I went was the front office. I wanted to get there before homeroom, but I hated walking past that demon statue up front. Instead, I walked around to the side entrance and practically ran to the office. The secretary, Mrs. White, gave me a weak smile when I walked through the door, and there were dark circles under her eyes.

"Good morning, dear. What can I help you with this morning?"

"I lost something Friday night at the football game," I said, my toe jiggling nervously inside my boot. "Did anyone turn in a necklace?"

"Oh, honey, I don't think so. It's just been a madhouse around here this morning, what with Tori's disappearance."

My eyes widened. "Tori Fairchild?"

"Yes, bless her heart," Mrs. White said. She brought the back of her hand up to her mouth and closed her eyes. After a few deep breaths, she opened them again and I saw that they were full of big, wet tears. "No one's seen her since the game Friday night. Half the town has been out looking for her since Sunday morning."

I stood there in shock, thinking about Tori and that guy after the game on Friday night. A guy who wasn't her boyfriend. Had he done something to her? Had Foster found out about them and gone crazy with jealousy? I swallowed hard.

"I'm sorry, what was it that you lost again?"

"A necklace," I said. "A silver chain with a blue sapphire pendant. But I can come back some other time." It seemed petty to be talking about a lost necklace when Tori was missing. What if something horrible happened to her?

"You're Harper, right? The new girl from Shadowford?"

I nodded and she wrote my name down on a yellow sticky pad along with a note about my necklace. "If anyone turns it in to the office, I'll make sure we let you know."

She stuck the yellow note onto a small cork board by her desk.

I thanked her and headed to my homeroom. The halls were filled with sobbing girls, somber faces, and clusters of students sharing whispered conversations. I rushed to homeroom, wondering if I should tell anyone about my midnight Tori sighting at the football stadium.

If I came forward with the information, Mrs. Shadowford would know I left the house after curfew to search the stadium. I had no doubt she would contact my case manager and send me straight to juvie. Then again, if I could help save Tori's life, wasn't that the most important thing? My mind ran circles around the issue. What if Tori had just run away with her new, possibly older boyfriend? Maybe she wasn't in trouble at all. Was I willing to risk my entire future for a girl that wasn't even the slightest bit civil to me? I felt certain she wouldn't have risked breaking a nail if it meant saving my life, so why did I even care?

For the first part of the morning, I played it safe. I kept my mouth shut and listened to the gossip around me.

"She was supposed to come to the party at Foster's parents' cabin by the lake Friday night, but she never showed," a brunette to my left was telling her friends.

"That's pretty typical Tori, though, right? To bail on a party?"

"Last year, maybe, but this year she's dating Foster. I don't think she'd ditch him at his own party."

"Well, what do you think happened to her?"

"I have no idea," the brunette said. "I just hope they find her and she's okay."

Then, in second period, I specifically sat near Allison Moore. If anyone knew about Tori's other man, it would be one of the cheerleaders. Allison's face was red and splotchy from crying.

"I can't believe this is happening," she cried to one of her fellow cheerleaders. I recognized the blonde she was talking to, but I didn't know her name. "We were the last two girls in the locker room, but I had to run home and get my sweatshirt cause it was getting chilly, right, so I left her and told her I'd meet her at the party."

"So she just never came home from the game or what?" the other girl asked in a whisper when the teacher turned her back.

"No one has seen or heard from her since I left the locker room Friday night." Allison's face scrunched up and she began to cry again. "I never should have left her alone in there. If something's happened to her, I'll never be able to forgive myself."

"It just doesn't make sense."

"Maybe someone abducted her from the school. It totally could have been some crazy stalker that, like, watched her at all the games or something," a petite girl with a short brown pixie cut said.

"The weirdest part is that the cops found her car parked on the street just a few blocks away from her own house," Allison said. "But she drove it to the game that night. If someone abducted her, why would they drive her car to the street where she lives and just leave it there?"

I strained to remember if I had seen Tori's car in the parking lot Friday night. I remembered that the lot seemed empty, no cars. I wondered if the cheerleaders had a special parking lot or if they parked in the main lot, but I didn't want to ask any questions that might raise suspicion.

By lunchtime, I had pretty much decided that if no word came in about Tori's whereabouts by the end of the school day, I would go to the police with my information. I still didn't know who the guy was that Tori was there with, but at least I could give them a description of his voice and what he was wearing. It would make for a record short time at a home for me, but I couldn't keep this secret to myself any longer.

I watched the clock for the rest of the afternoon, feeling as if each second that went by brought me closer to my own deathbed. Then, minutes before the bell that would seal my fate, the news came in.

Tori Fairchild's body had been found.

YOU'LL NEED TO
COME WITH US

TORI FAIRCHILD'S BODY had been discovered in the woods near her house at approximately two pm that afternoon.

News spread through the school like wildfire. Officers from the local sheriff's department knocked on the door of my seventh period English class roughly ten minutes after the news hit. Mrs. King, my English teacher, talked quietly with a tall, gray-haired officer for a few moments in the hallway, then entered the room with a pale face. To my surprise, she was looking directly at me.

"Harper Madison, the officers outside would like to talk to you."

Her words pierced through me. Did they know about my secret? Had someone seen me at the stadium that night? I was unable to move, frozen to the seat of my desk.

"Harper?" Mrs. King called my name louder. Her voice had an edge of hysteria to it. No doubt she'd been really close to Tori, being her cheer coach and all. I couldn't imagine what she was going through.

Every pair of eyes was on me. Probably wondering what in the world the new Shadowford freak had to do with Tori's death. Hell, I was wondering that myself. It was possible I had been one of the last people to see her alive, but no one actually knew that.

Unless I'd been wrong and the guy out there with her saw my face.

Slowly, I stood and gathered my things. Outside the classroom, I faced the two officers. "I'm Harper Madison," I said.

"You'll need to come with us," the older man said.

"Why?" My mouth went completely dry and I had a hard time swallowing. "What's wrong?"

"I can't discuss the details of the case out here in the hallway of the public school. As long as you cooperate, we'll do you the favor of not handcuffing you here in front of your friends."

Handcuffing? Jesus, what were they saying? That I was a suspect? The world around me began to spin uncontrollably. I shook my head.

"No, I didn't do anything wrong. I don't understand what's going on here."

My entire body went cold and my stomach lurched. The younger officer, a middle-aged man with a beer belly and a bushy mustache, grabbed my upper arm and began to pull me down the hall. He pinched my skin a bit, his fingers digging into my arm as I shuffled reluctantly toward the front entryway.

The bright afternoon sun hit me full in the face as we pushed through the front doors. I jerked my arm away from the policeman and stepped back from him. He made a move toward me like he was ready to catch me if I decided to run, but he relaxed when he saw that I wasn't exactly trying to make a break for it.

"I can walk just fine on my own," I said. But as I made my way past the tall demon statue, I felt the same wave of dizziness

I'd felt on my first day of school. I stumbled slightly, then recovered.

"You okay?" the older man asked.

No, I wanted to say. I am most definitely not okay.

Instead, I nodded my head and walked obediently to the waiting squad car. This wasn't my first time in the back of a police car. I hated that feeling of being out of control. Locked away like an animal with no way to escape. It scared me to think what an actual prison cell must feel like. I hoped to God I wasn't about to find out.

The Peachville police station was a tiny building in the center of downtown. A young officer sat at the front desk in the small reception area. He didn't look much older than me with his fresh haircut and smooth baby face. As we entered the room, he stood quickly, knocking over a full jar of pencils.

"Oh shoot." He scrambled to pick them up, but a few pencils rolled off the desk top and onto the floor. "Sorry sir."

"Ellis, what did Sheriff Hollingsworth tell you about those damn pencils?" the older officer said.

"I know sir, I just-"

"Just clean 'em up and escort this young woman into an interrogation room. I don't have time for your crap today. We've got a serious investigation to take care of."

Ellis bent over to retrieve the escaped pencils, then turned his attention to me. "Let's go."

"Lead the way," I said.

He brought me down a narrow hallway, then led me to a small room that held a single desk and two metal folding chairs. Plastic flooring curled up at the edges of the room and sad, faded yellow curtains covered a single grimy window. From the way the rest of the town looked with its brick sidewalks and landscaped parks, I hadn't expected the police department to be so rundown and dreary. Maybe a small town like this didn't see enough crime to warrant a fancy police station.

"Want a soda or somethin'?" Ellis asked.

"No thanks," I said. I just wanted someone to tell me what the hell I was doing there. Plus, I wasn't totally sure I'd be able to swallow. Every muscle in my body was tense.

They left me alone in that small, slightly smelly room for over half an hour before a petite black woman finally came in. By then, I'd practically chewed off all my fingernails.

She was dressed in a navy suit with a white button down shirt. She didn't look like she belonged in a place like this, and I wondered if she was from DFCS like Mrs. Meeks. She slapped a yellow folder down on the desk in front of me, then sat down.

"Harper Madison. Sixteen years old. Adopted at birth by Heath and Jill Madison of Gwinnett County, Georgia. At the age of eight, your adoptive father was killed in a house fire. A fire that Jill Madison claims you started on purpose."

"That's not true," I said.

"Which part?" the woman asked.

"The fire," I said. "It was an accident." And why did that matter now? What did any of this have to do with Tori Fairchild?

"The state fire marshal's investigation was inconclusive. According to his notes, the fire was unusual in that it did not have a single point of origin. Rather, he thought it seemed as though fire sprang up in several places simultaneously."

That last bit she read directly from my file. She paused and flipped through several more pages, then looked up, her eyes meeting mine for the first time. She had caramel-colored eyes that were almost hypnotic. I wanted to look away, but I couldn't.

"You've had a long string of foster homes ever since then, is that correct?"

I nodded. I had lost count, there were so many. It wasn't an easy thing to think about.

"And why do you think that is, Miss Madison?"

I forced my gaze away from hers and she stood up. She paced the room, waiting for an answer to her question. I wasn't sure how to answer her.

"Why do you think that fifteen different foster homes in the Atlanta area had such a problem with you that they refused to house you any longer? According to your file, you never stayed in one place longer than six months. Why?" She raised her voice and moved to stand very close to me.

I leaned my elbows on the desk in front of me and rested my head in my hands. How was I supposed to answer a question like that? Admit that I was a freak? "I thought you guys brought me here to talk about Tori," I said.

"We will talk about whatever I tell you we're going to talk about," the woman said, placing her hands on the table and leaning so close to my face I could smell the cinnamon in her gum. "Tell me why you were kicked out of your latest foster home in Atlanta."

I ground my teeth together and turned my head away. It was one thing to talk to Mrs. Meeks about these things. I had known her since I was eight years old. Since the fire. But this woman? She hadn't so much as told me her name or who she worked for.

"Fine, you want to know who I am?" she said. "My name is Sheriff Daneka Hollingsworth."

My face flushed. How had she known I was wondering about her name? I swallowed. "I don't want to talk about it."

"This isn't about what you want," she said. "Now talk."

The look in her eyes scared me. It was like she could see through me. Into me.

"We didn't get along."

"Be more specific."

"I was only there for a couple of weeks," I started. "They fought all the time. And when they would fight, the lady, Pat, she would always come into our room and take it out on us."

"Who else was there with you?"

"A couple of younger kids. Joy and Ashley. They were in sixth grade. We all shared a room with bunk beds."

"So what happened the night you got kicked out?"

A bead of sweat formed on my lip and I swiped it away. "I don't know. Nothing. They didn't want me there anymore."

I wondered how much the file in the Sheriff's hands said about me. I didn't want to tell her anything about my past, but I had the feeling she wasn't going to give me a choice.

"Don't lie to me or you'll be sorry."

I hugged my arms close to my body, then spoke. "They'd had a really bad fight earlier at dinner, so I was expecting her to come after us as usual. Well, just before bedtime, Pat comes into our room yelling about how the house is a mess and it's all our fault. How we don't appreciate what she's doing for us. The younger girls were already dressed and in bed, but Pat grabbed Joy by the hair and pulled her from the bed."

"How did that make you feel?"

"Angry," I said. "Helpless. I got down from the top bunk and told her to stop picking on the younger girls. She shoved Joy to the side and came at me like she was going to hit me. I guess I just freaked out."

"What happened?" The sheriff came back around to her chair and sat across from me. Her eyes were locked on my face.

"I don't know." I was so afraid to tell her the truth.

"Tell me," she said. "Something happened that night that you couldn't control. Tell me what it was."

I took a deep breath. "It was like anger was boiling inside of me. Like it had a life of its own, in a way. I felt all of that anger sort of focus in on her and everything else in the room went blurry. Before I knew it, some of the things on the side table..." I couldn't go on. How could I explain what happened that night? She'd think I was crazy and lock me up for sure. I wasn't even sure why I'd told her this much, but I couldn't seem to help myself.

"They rose up from the desk?" she asked, her voice excited. "Like they were flying around the room, right?"

I stared back at her, heart racing in my chest. I thought of Mrs. Meeks words to me that night. "No, that's insane," I said. "Things don't fly around the room on their own."

"I told you not to lie to me. The lamp on the desk." She narrowed her eyes at me, then tilted her head slightly. "You hit her with it."

"No," I said. "I didn't do it on purpose. You don't understand-"

"Oh I understand. You were angry. And when you get angry, you move things with your mind, don't you Harper? You're different from other people, aren't you?"

I hung my head down. How did she know all this? I waited for her to say I was some kind of witch who deserved to be punished. A freak who belonged in an institution.

"That night, your anger was focused on Pat Sanders. That's why the lamp hit her. You might not have known you were doing it, but it was you that hit her with that lamp, Harper."

I looked away. "I..."

"Sometimes, it's fire, isn't it?"

I shook my head. "No."

"Yes. Just like with Heath and Jill Madison when you were eight years old. When you let your anger get out of control, you start fires and burn people."

"No," I said again, louder. "That's not what happened."

"And that's what happened with Tori Fairchild on Friday night, isn't it?"

My eyes widened. "You think I killed Tori? I would never do something like that."

"You just told me you hit a woman in the head with a lamp when you were angry with her," she said. She slammed her hands down on the desk and I jumped back, frightened. "And you killed your adoptive father when you were eight."

"No, I told you I didn't mean to do it."

"Then maybe you didn't mean to do this either." She flipped three pictures over and slid them toward me. "Maybe Tori just made you angry. She was burned alive, Harper. Cooked from the inside."

The pictures were gruesome. Tori's body was burned and bloody. I brought my hand to my mouth and looked away, shutting my eyes tight. "Oh, God."

"Look at these pictures, Harper. Look at what you did!"

"I didn't do that," I said. I felt like I was going to throw up. How could someone think I was capable of such a horrible thing? The images of Tori's blackened skin were horrifying.

The sheriff came around to my side of the table and stood behind me. She placed her hands on my head and forced my face straight down toward where the pictures lay spread on the table. In my ear, she said, "Then why was she holding your necklace in her hand?"

NO ONE EVER BELIEVED

Y STOMACH CLENCHED as I forced myself to look at the pictures of Tori's body. I kept my eyes focused on the part of one picture that showed her hands up close. My eyes widened as I saw what Sheriff Hollingsworth was talking about. My mother's sapphire necklace was tangled around Tori's limp right hand.

I couldn't speak. Where would she have gotten the necklace? It was possible she picked it up at the field that night, but why? She didn't seem like the type of person who would pick up a random necklace off the ground and keep it with her. None of this made sense. My mind spun.

I pushed the pictures away from me. I didn't want to look at them anymore.

"Here's what I think happened," Sheriff Hollingsworth said, sitting half on top of the desk in front of me. "You're a troubled girl who lets things get out of control when she's angry. You move to Shadowford against your will and on your first day of school, you have a run-in with the most popular girl in the sophomore class. She humiliates you in front of the entire school."

I listened in horror. This woman actually believed I was capable of murder. I wanted to stop her. To tell her to shut up. But I couldn't speak. My lips were pressed tight together, and my legs were trembling slightly.

This can't be happening.

"You follow her back to her house on Friday night after the game. Lure her into the woods where you get into another argument. Things get heated and you lose control. You burn her, but Tori fights back and manages to pull your necklace from your neck. Scared, you run off, leaving her there in the woods to die."

"No," I said. My voice came out weak and dry. "I wouldn't do something like that."

"But you did have an argument with Tori Fairchild?"

"In the lunchroom that day, yes. But I didn't follow her on Friday night," I said. "And you're wrong about the necklace. I lost it at the game on Friday. Ask Ella Mae or any of the other girls. I went back to look for it after the game, but I couldn't find it."

"So you admit that the necklace Tori has clutched in her hands is yours?"

Shit. Am I messing up here? I felt trapped.

"Are you allowed to question me without a lawyer? Or at least legal guardian. I'm still a minor," I said, throwing my chin up and folding my arms across my chest. I was trying to seem tough, but think I ended up looking more like a scared kid.

"Where do you think you are? Atlanta?" The sheriff laughed and it sent chills down my spine. "I can do whatever I want with you and no one will ever believe I did anything wrong. You don't exactly have a track record for telling the truth and being a good girl."

I clutched the sleeve of my shirt into a tight fist, trying not to panic. She was right, though. No one would believe me. No one ever believed me.

The Sheriff pulled out a yellow sticky note and placed it on the table. It was the secretary's note from this morning with my name and a description of the necklace. "It's alright, you don't have to answer that question anyway. We know the necklace is yours. We have witnesses that saw you wearing it. Mrs. King for one. Agnes, your friend at Shadowford. And there's a notebook in your bedroom with a drawing of a woman wearing it. Your mother, I'm guessing."

"You've been going through my things?" I felt betrayed. Helpless.

"Tell me what really happened on Friday night," she said.

I knew I had to tell her about sneaking out and seeing Tori with the boy on the field, but someone knocked on the door before I had the chance.

"Sheriff?" Ellis poked his head just inside the door.

A flash of anger crossed the Sheriff's face. "What?"

"The mayor wants to see you real quick. She says it's important."

Sheriff Hollingsworth's eyes widened. She straightened her jacket and walked to the open door. Almost as an afterthought, she turned back to me. "Don't move."

The door closed behind her and I let out a huge breath. Hot tears threatened my eyes, and I slouched down low in my chair. If they charged me with Tori's murder, they would send me someplace much worse than juvenile detention. I shuddered.

I looked up as the door opened once more. An Asian woman smiled at me from the doorway. She had the most beautiful straight black hair that fell below her shoulders, and her eyes were like black glass. "Harper, I'm Mayor Chen."

Lark's mother. I remembered Agnes telling me she was the mayor's daughter. I had wrongly assumed the mayor was a man.

"I just have a couple of questions for you, if that's okay?" Her voice was soft and smooth. Comforting.

I nodded, relaxing slightly.

"Where did you get the sapphire pendant?"

"It was my mother's," I said.

"But you were adopted, correct?"

I nodded. "As a baby. But my adoptive parents, they gave me the necklace when I turned eight. That's when they first told me that I was adopted. They said my mother's only request was that they made sure I got that necklace."

Mayor Chen seemed to think this over for a moment, then turned back to me. "Do you know anything else about your real mother?"

Why was she asking me about my mother? And the necklace? What did any of this have to do with Tori's death? I shook my head slightly. "I don't know much," I said.

"But you've seen her before?"

"Not really. I mean, I accidentally saw a picture of her that my adoptive parents kept in a file in their desk."

"And that's how you knew to draw that picture we found in your notebook? Of her wearing the necklace?"

I nodded again.

"Do you have any idea how Tori Fairchild would have gotten hold of your necklace?"

"No, that's what I was trying to tell the sheriff. I lost that necklace Friday night at the game. I always wear it, every day. But when I was getting in the van to come home that night, it was gone. It had to have fallen off somewhere at the stadium. Anyone could have picked it up."

Mayor Chen's eyes locked onto mine, and I searched them, hoping to see some sign that she believed me. On the table, the folder fluttered closed. Mayor Chen hadn't even moved her hand. I stared down at the closed folder, then back up at her ebony eyes.

"Miss Madison, thank you for your cooperation today," she said. "You are free to go."

IS THAT YOU?

*E*LLIS DROVE ME home in his squad car. This time, I got to ride up front.

"How you hangin' in there?" he asked. "Seems like they kinda gave you a rough time in there."

I sank deeper in my seat. "I guess I'm alright." I didn't really want to talk about it with this guy.

"They can be kind of rough on me too," he said.

I figured he was just trying to make me feel better, but when I looked over at him, I could see honesty in his face. The older man had been kind of mean to him when he dropped those pencils. Maybe he knew what it felt like to never have anyone take you seriously.

"What's with the sheriff?" I asked.

"What do ya mean?"

"Small town like this. I guess I wasn't expecting a pretty petite lady to be the boss around here. It was sorta unexpected."

"Oh," he said with a shrug. "I guess I never really thought about it that much. Sheriff Hollingsworth might be small, but she's tough. Real tough. And smart too."

"It's just that in the movies and stuff, you always see towns like this with old white guys in charge. The good ol' boys. But here, I don't know. This town is very... progressive. Black lady sheriff. Asian woman mayor. Lots of minority women in charge. All very beautiful." I don't know why I was talking to Ellis about these things. It was more that I was just working out my own questions and he just happened to be there. But now that I did take a moment to think about it, having all these women in power did seem a little unusual.

Mayor Chen is like me.

The realization had come to me the second she closed that folder, but I didn't want to admit it. What did that even mean? She was like me. So what? Wasn't that a good thing? But somehow it didn't feel good. It felt dangerous.

Ellis looked confused. His eyebrows were drawn together and his lips were turned down in a concentrated frown. "I never really considered it," he mumbled.

I started to think about who else might be powerful in this town. There was old Mrs. Shadowford, but she didn't seem to hold much sway in the political arena. Still, she was obviously wealthy and owned a lot of property. Her teacup had rattled when she got angry. I shivered.

Principal Tate at the high school was a woman. Drake's sister owned the most popular shop in town. If I asked around, I wonder how many more women I could find in high places.

Officer Ellis pulled down the drive toward Shadowford and my palms grew sweaty. I had no idea what to expect from Ella Mae and Mrs. Shadowford. Would they kick me out? Or were they going to be lenient since Mayor Chen excused me from the investigation?

The only thing I was sure of was that I needed to get to Jackson Hunt before he told anyone what he saw the night that Tori died. If anyone found out I had left the house around midnight, I would be tossed right back into the Sheriff's office, and this time, things might not turn out so well.

"Can you drop me off here at the end of the driveway?" I asked.

Officer Ellis slowed to a halt and considered my question. "No can do," he said. "I mean, the sheriff told me to make sure you got home safely. I don't think it's such a good idea for me to drop you off back here. It's getting pretty dark out there."

"Please," I said, begging. "Do you know how embarrassing it will be to have a squad car drop me off in front of the house? All the girls will see me, and everyone will make a big fuss out of it. But if you drop me off here, I can sneak around back and talk to Mrs. Shadowford directly, without having to try to explain to the other girls what happened today. I promise, I'll go straight inside."

I could tell he was uncertain about what to do, but as I suspected, he was easily swayed. Not the brightest crayon in the box. "Alright, but I'm gonna sit right here at the edge of the driveway and make sure you get around the back of the house okay."

"Thank you so much," I said, pulling off my seat-belt and bolting from the car before he could change his mind. I practically ran all the way down the driveway, sticking close to the edge of the treeline so that no one inside could see me. Hopefully the police car was far enough down the drive that no one had seen his lights.

When I made it to the edge of the house, I turned and waved to Officer Ellis. He flicked his lights at me once, then backed up and pulled off. As fast as I could, I sprinted to the overgrown garden, avoiding the automatic light over the barn. The weeds were so high, I had to walk slowly and carefully, but at least the shadows kept me hidden from view. In a few minutes, I came through the other side and found myself near the back of the Hunt's house.

A light in one of the back rooms shone through the darkness and I tiptoed my way toward the window. Ella Mae was inside at her sewing machine, a TV on across the room. I backed away slowly, careful not to trip over anything, then continued on along the back of the one story house. Two windows were dark, then at the end, a dull amber glow.

Jackson sat in his room, leaning over his desk. He was shirtless, wearing only his tattered jeans. My stomach fluttered. His bare, tan back was smooth and muscular. I hesitated for a moment, noticing a long, red scar across his side. It was strangely beautiful and brought a sudden sadness to my heart.

I pulled myself together and knocked on the glass.

Jackson's head snapped up and he squinted toward me. I waved and motioned for him to open it so we could talk.

"Harper, is that you?"

"Yes," I whispered through the screen. "No one knows I'm home yet. I really need to talk to you, can you come outside?"

He glanced toward his work at the desk and a strange look crossed his face. Disappointment?

"I'm sorry if I'm interrupting something important, but this is really serious."

"I know," he said. "It's not that. It's just... hang on."

He pulled the window up as far as it would go, then unlatched the screen from its hooks. "Grab this," he said.

I helped him take the screen off of the window, then took his hand as he pulled me into his room. I stumbled slightly as I stood up, leaning against his bare chest for support. My knees went weak and I suddenly felt extra aware of what I must look like. My hair was wild from running and my shoes were slightly muddy from the garden. I ran a hand through my hair and begged my heart to stop racing.

"Are you okay?" Jackson let go of my hand, but didn't move away. I could smell his soap, woodsy and natural. The scar on his side wrapped around the front of his body. I wondered what in the world happened to have caused such an ugly scar. Warmth radiated from his bare skin, and I wanted to move closer. I wanted to run my hand along the mark.

Instead, I took a step back. "Yeah. I'm sure you heard what happened, right?"

He nodded. "It's a small town. Word travels fast around here."

"I figured." I stepped around him and sat down on his bed, feeling light headed and unsure on my feet. "It was weird. They brought me in for questioning, railed on me, practically accused me of murdering Tori."

"Then what?"

"Then they just let me go. The mayor came in and asked me all these questions about my necklace, then told me I was free to go."

"Your necklace?" He sat down in his desk chair, then rolled it over near me.

"It's this sapphire pendant I always wear. It was my mother's. And it's the reason I was out that night you saw me in the barn. The night Tori died," I said. "I lost it at the game, so I snuck out of my room to go look for it at the stadium."

"Why did they want to know about that?"

I told him all about the origins of the necklace and exactly what the police had told me about Tori's death. Jackson listened with an intense concentration.

"I came to you before I went back to the house, because I didn't know when I'd have another chance to talk to you. I have no idea if they're going to let me stay here or send me away to another place. It's all up in the air." I looked up into his eyes. "You can't tell anyone you saw me that night. If they find out, they'll arrest me. But I didn't kill her. I swear to God, I wouldn't do something like that."

"I know you wouldn't." He took my hand in his. "I told you your secret is safe with me, remember?"

I let out a nervous sigh. "Thank you."

Silence filled the room and everything in my body focused in on that one spot of my hand where he was touching me.

"Can I ask you something?"

"Sure," he said.

"How did you know Tori? I mean, I know you were in school together, but there was more to it than that, right?"

He tilted his head to the side, then sat back in his chair, pulling his hand away. "Why do you say that?"

"Because I saw you. My first night at Shadowford. You were out by the garden with her and you wouldn't give her something she wanted. I thought you saw me there, in the window."

He ran his hand through his hair. "I thought I felt someone watching us, but I wasn't sure."

I waited for him to answer my question.

"I think there's something you should see," he said.

He turned to grab the notebook he'd been drawing in. He stared down at it for a moment, then turned it around to show me. There, drawn on the paper, was a pencil sketch of me, standing in a room full of flames.

THIS TOWN ISN'T LIKE OTHER PLACES

"*I* DON'T UNDERSTAND."

My hands trembled as I held the drawing.

"I can't explain it exactly," Jackson said. "Sometimes I see things. I don't know when or where these images will come to me, and most of the time I don't know what the images mean until..." his voice trailed off. He stood and began to pace the room.

I swallowed. "Until what?"

"You wouldn't believe me even if I told you." He ran a hand through his hair. Normally, he wore it slightly spiked up in the front, but today it fell across his forehead and into his eyes, making him seem softer somehow.

The image was drawn on the plain white paper of the notebook. There was nothing special about it except the image itself. He had drawn it with a charcoal pencil and the level of detail was astonishing. At first glance, it looked only like a girl, me, standing in a room filled with flames. Look closer, though, and there was so much more.

A dark figure stood behind me in the shadows, a single lightning bolt moving across its face. And there, so consumed in flame I could hardly make it out, I saw the form of a demon. He was coming straight for me. There was something so familiar about the demon's face. Part gargoyle, part human. Its presence in the picture made me feel creepy and unsettled to the point of almost feeling paralyzed.

"You have to tell me, Jackson." My voice came out more demanding than I intended, but I had to know. "What does this picture mean?"

He stopped pacing, his back to me as he spoke again. "These drawings are of the future, Harper." He turned and our eyes met. "Whatever I draw always comes true, and it usually happens within days. Maybe a week. Maybe two if we're lucky."

My heart stopped beating for a moment. My breath caught in my throat and I looked down at the page. Was this a picture of my own death?

"No." I stood and slammed the paper against his chest. "This is ridiculous. No one can see the future. I was in a fire once when I was little. You must have heard your mother talking about it or something, so this is what came out when you sat down to draw. I am not going to die in fire. Not tomorrow. Not next week. Not ever."

Jackson took the notebook from me and flipped several pages back. "I know it's hard to believe," he said. "Here."

He handed me the drawings and I gasped. I shook my head furiously. There, on the page, was a drawing of Tori Fairchild, still in her Demons uniform. Her body was burned and contorted, almost exactly in the same pose as the pictures I'd seen of her death. I turned it over on the bed and tried to control the growing nausea in my stomach.

"I'm sorry to have to show you that, Harper, but I'm afraid for you," he said. "I'm not supposed to share stuff like this with anyone. I learned a long time ago that I can't change the stuff in these drawings. I don't even know why I told you. There's just something about you, Harper. I wanted to, I don't know, help you. I wanted to do something for once instead of just stand by and watch it happen."

My breath came in quick, shallow bursts and my heart raced.

"I gotta get out of here," I said, pushing past him.

Jackson grabbed my arm and pulled me toward him. His body was warm and tense against mine and I cursed myself for being so damn attracted to him. I yanked my arm to get away, but he held me tight until I stopped struggling and looked up into his warm green eyes.

"You don't understand," he said. "This town isn't like other places. I wish I could explain it to you, but I'm bound by an oath older than time. I'm already taking a risk by showing you this picture, but I don't want anything to happen to you. Maybe together we can find a way to stop this from coming true, but I need you to believe me."

His eyes pleaded with mine and something inside of me softened. I knew how he felt. Every time I tried to explain the strange things that happened in my life, people turned their back on me, refusing to listen to what I had to say. There were times when I didn't want to admit it, but there was something different about me. Something I couldn't control. But in this town, I wasn't the only one who was different. Deep down, I'd known it since the minute I first laid eyes on Shadowford.

My body relaxed and he loosened his grip on my arm. He pulled me close in a tight hug. I laid my head on his bare chest and breathed in the masculine scent of him. My arms circled around his waist, loose at first, then tighter. Jackson took my shoulders in his hands and leaned me back slightly. Nervously, I tilted my chin up toward his face.

"Harper," he whispered.

His lips slowly descended on mine and I rose up to meet him. He kissed me softly and the room around me felt as if it were spinning. A shiver ran up my spine as his hand moved to the back of my neck, urging me closer. My lips parted and our kiss deepened.

I pressed my body closer, lifting slightly onto my tiptoes and bringing my arms up around his neck. In that moment, we existed on a higher plane. I kept my eyes closed and felt him melt into me. A low groan sounded at the back of his throat, creating a strange need inside of me I had never felt before. My knees felt weak, my head light.

When he finally pulled away, I felt that the entire world had changed. I nuzzled my face against his chest.

"What do we do now?" I asked.

"We keep you safe," he said, kissing the top of my head.

I didn't understand everything that was going on in this strange town. I had no idea if the picture he'd drawn would really come true. But I knew he wouldn't lie to me. And I knew that he would be there for me. Some wall between us had come crashing down.

There in his arms, I felt safer than I ever dreamed I could.

SIT DOWN, GIRL

OUTSIDE, THE NIGHT air was crisp and cool. Lights were on throughout the main house. I came around the house and entered through the front door as if I had just gotten home. The idea of going straight up to my room and attempting to ignore the fact that I had been questioned by the police was pretty inviting, but in the end, I decided it was better to face Mrs. Shadowford and get the whole thing over with.

I walked to the door to her suite of rooms feeling like it was a walk to my own execution. How long would it take Mrs. Meeks to arrange a spot for me at the juvenile detention center? A day? An hour?

I knocked on the thick wooden door and waited.

"Yes?" Mrs. Shadowford's voice was muffled.

I leaned close to the door. "It's Harper."

"Come in," she said. She didn't sound excited to have me back, and for the first time, I realized it was strange that no one from Shadowford had come to the police station to support me. Shouldn't someone have come for me? After all, these people were my guardians.

A sickening dread entered my heart as I opened the door and crossed over the threshold over her office. I hadn't been in that room since my first day at Shadowford. It seemed darker in here than any of the other rooms in the house. And colder.

Mrs. Shadowford sat behind her desk. She looked up as I entered, her face stern, lips pursed.

"I didn't hear a car drive up," she said. "Who brought you home?"

"Officer Ellis dropped me off." I didn't explain further.

She eyed me curiously. "The mayor called me. She told me about what you had to go through today, and I'm terribly sorry they put you through all that for nothing. I told her it's obvious you weren't involved in the death of that poor girl. But I do wonder how she got hold of that necklace of yours."

I stood and stared at her, unsure how I was expected to respond. I certainly had no idea how Tori got my necklace.

"Sit down, girl. Don't stand there staring at me like no one ever taught you any manners."

I sat across from her in a burgundy leather chair. Its seat was cracked and worn, and the springs inside squeaked as I sat down. "Are you going to kick me out of Shadowford?" I asked.

"Did you do something wrong?" She narrowed her eyes at me.

"No. But I thought-"

"If you didn't break any rules, then I don't see a need to let you go," she said. "Calm down, girl, and have some water. You look like you're about to pass out."

She had an ivory teacup on the desk in front of her and filled it with water from an open water bottle in her desk. She pushed the cup toward me and nodded expectantly. With trembling hands, I took the cup and raised it to my lips. The water tasted sweet and smelled faintly like rose-petals. I took only a slight sip, then set the cup down.

"Thank you."

"Fine, fine," she said. "I'm sure you're exhausted after such a tough day. Why don't you go on upstairs and get ready for bed. We can talk about this in the morning. It's possible the authorities will want to talk to you again, but I feel confident that they have ruled you out as a suspect."

Her words weren't comforting. There was an impersonal edge to her voice that made me feel uneasy.

I managed to avoid the other girls on the way up to my room. As soon as I was closed inside, I wedged my shoe under the door and went into the bathroom to wash my face. I let the water run in the sink until it was hot and steam poured into the room. I was so tired all of a sudden. My legs felt like jelly and the light was brighter than I remembered it. Shaking it off as best I could, I leaned down to splash water on my face. When I came up, the world went fuzzy.

I steadied myself against the sink and closed my eyes. I was just tired, that was all. It had been a long day. An emotional day. I just needed some sleep. But when I opened my eyes again, my vision was worse. I could barely make out my own image in the mirror. I reached over and rubbed at it with my hand, wiping away the steam, but I lost my balance and stumbled backward against the wall.

Panic seized me as my legs gave out. I fell to the floor. My face smacked against the cold, hard tile. My eyelids were so heavy. I fought it as hard as I could, but the darkness won out, pulling me into its arms and dragging me under.

I MUST BE DREAMING

*M*Y ENTIRE BODY burned with fever. I curled into a little ball and begged for it to stop. My eyelids felt like they were glued shut and sweat slid down the back of my neck. Inside my head, my thoughts swam around in circles, never finding a clear focus. I couldn't tell if I was awake or asleep and every time I almost climbed up into consciousness, the darkness would pull me back down.

Where was I?

My eyes fluttered open slightly, then closed again. It was dark. The sound of water dripped in the distance, almost echoing in my head as though I were inside a cave. Or a dungeon.

I must be dreaming.

There was no sense of time. There was only the endless trembling of my body against a cold, hard surface.

The sound of chanting jarred me awake. A light rose up in the darkness. A single flame. Someone took my hand and it was so warm. I opened my mouth to ask them for a blanket, but I didn't have a voice. I tried to swallow but my mouth felt like a sea of sand.

I saw the glint of silver overhead, then felt a searing pain on my palm. I tried to jerk away. To sit up. To cry out. But I was powerless and weak. Warm blood trickled down my hand and onto my wrist and the chanting continued. In the dim light, a woman with flowing black hair stood over me. Her face was covered with a shiny black mask. Her eyes glowed a deep crimson.

"She is the one," the woman said. "The Prima has finally come home."

The chanting grew louder all around me. It took every ounce of my strength to open my eyes wider and lift my head. Dark shadows swirled around the room like bats and I cried out in fear.

The woman put her hand over my eyes and my world went black. A flash of events passed behind my darkened lids, pulled from within me. Mrs. Shadowford's rattling teacup. Screams in the middle of the night. Fainting near the statue. Losing my necklace.

Panic reached up to tear at my throat. I wanted it to stop, but had no control. Tori at the stadium that night. Being questioned at the station. Meeting Lark's mother. And Jackson. His kiss was warm on my lips, then gone in an instant. Each memory slipped through my brain like water through my fingertips.

Is this what it's like to die?

I felt the cool comfort of my sapphire pendant as it was placed around my neck. I lifted my hand to the stone, then surrendered to the shadows.

I WASN'T SUPPOSED TO FORGET

*L*IGHT STREAMED IN through the open curtains, and I pulled the comforter over my head to block the pain of it.

"Harper? Are you awake?"

Reluctantly, I pushed aside the fabric and squinted up at the figure above my bed. "Agnes?"

"You're awake! How are you feeling?" Agnes didn't wait for an answer. Her footsteps clattered across the room toward the door. "Ella Mae? Harper's awake!"

More footsteps on the stairs. I closed my eyes. Simply opening them made me tired. The inside of my head felt dense and fuzzy, as if someone had stuffed a thousand cotton balls inside.

"Harper, honey, how are you feeling?" Ella Mae this time. Her worried face appeared as she sat down in a chair next to my bed. She placed a cool wet cloth on my forehead.

"That feels nice," I said. My voice didn't sound like my own. It was scratchy and hoarse. What the hell happened to me? The last thing I remembered...I couldn't even figure out what was real and what wasn't. Thinking about it too hard sent a stab of pain through my temple.

"We were so worried about you. You have no idea," Agnes said. She sat at the foot of the bed and placed her hand on my covered feet.

"Here, drink some water." Ella Mae propped me up on a bunch of pillows, then handed me a small glass of ice water.

The water was so cold on my throat it almost burned. "Thank you," I said. Some of the raspy sound was already gone. I cleared my throat and drank some more.

"There is so much to tell you," Agnes said. She bounced a little on the bed and the room went temporarily spinning.

I pressed my hands against the mattress, trying to make it stop.

"Agnes, stop bouncing. You're gonna make her sick," Ella Mae said.

When I opened my eyes, I noticed Courtney had joined Agnes at the foot of the bed. She smiled shyly up at me, her blonde hair falling into her face. Mary Anne stood silently in the doorway. When I looked her way, she turned and left.

"What happened to me?" I asked.

"You've been sick with the flu," Ella Mae said, replacing the warm cloth on my head with a fresh cool one. She put a thermometer in my mouth and told me to keep my mouth closed. "You've been in here running in and out of sleep for the past five days."

"Five days," I mumbled, talking around the thermometer. How could I have been sleeping for nearly an entire week? I suddenly felt very hot. Almost claustrophobic. Why couldn't I remember what happened? I threw the covers off my legs and tried to stand up.

"Calm down," Ella Mae said. "You don't want to wear yourself out when you just woke up. Agnes, go down to the kitchen and get some juice and toast."

The room spun violently and I fell back onto the pillows. Ella Mae lifted my legs onto the bed and covered them back up. I was so incredibly tired, but I knew it was important that I remember. But remember what? I closed my eyes and tried to think. School. Something terrible happened. Tori Fairchild was dead. I remembered sitting in class when the news came about her death. But then what? Everything grew dim after that. I lifted my hand up to touch my mother's sapphire pendant.

For a moment, I was worried it wouldn't be there. But that was silly, right? I always wore her necklace. At the back of my mind, though, a memory tugged at me.

But the necklace was there where I expected it to be. I curled my fingers around it and ran the pendant back and forth along the silver chain.

Ella Mae took the thermometer from my mouth and shook her head. "You've still got a fever, but it's not as bad as it was before. I think you're still going to need a couple of days at home before you go back to school. I'll talk to Mrs. Shadowford about it. You just rest up, okay? Agnes'll bring you something to eat, and I want you to try and get something down. You need to start building your strength up again."

I nodded and closed my eyes. Sleep threatened to suck me back down, but I knew there was something more to remember. Something important that I wasn't supposed to forget. But it wouldn't come to me.

Behind my eyelids, all I could see was the glowing light of a single candle. I heard voices chanting. A silver knife sliced into my hand. I gasped and sat up in bed, eyes wide open. The room was darker now that the sun had gone down. Agnes had left the juice and toast on the side table by my bed, but that must have been hours ago. Had I been dreaming?

I lifted my hand. A fresh bandage was taped around my palm. With my other hand, I pulled off the tape and unwrapped the gauze. There, in the middle of my palm, still throbbing slightly, was a diagonal cut that ran the length of my hand.

CLAIRE

I SPENT THE REST of the weekend in bed. On the following Monday, the other girls were at school during the day and Ella Mae had stuff to do around the house, so I stayed in my room or went downstairs to play games on the laptop. My body slowly recovered from the illness. With each day, I could feel my strength returning.

By day three, I was bored out of my mind. I started to roam around the mansion, looking at which books they had on the shelves and what paintings were on the walls. Since I had first come to Shadowford, I hadn't spent much time looking around and really paying attention to the house itself. It was by far the most beautiful place I had ever lived. And it was huge.

The first floor was pretty boring as far as exploration goes. Since I wasn't allowed into Mrs. Shadowford's suite of rooms, that left the same old rooms we all moved around in every day. I glanced up the narrow staircase leading to the third floor and bit my lip. Ella Mae had told me not to go up there, but she was all the way downstairs and no one was home.

I stepped gingerly onto the staircase and made my way up to the door. One of the stairs near the top creaked and I froze, waiting to see if Ella Mae would call out to me. When she didn't, I kept going. At the top, I pushed open the painted blue door and glanced inside. There was only a single room up there, and it was full of old boxes. Why would they care if anyone came up here? Not finding any big secret, I went back downstairs.

The second floor was more interesting. In addition to the four bedrooms us girls stayed in, there were four other empty bedrooms.

In the first empty room, I didn't find anything of interest. Dust. That was pretty much it. But the second room was a different story. At first, it seemed like the other. Dusty and ancient. The floral bedspread was perfectly made up. The windows were shut tight. But when I sat down on the bed, I felt the sudden urge to look under it. I got down on my hands and knees. When I lifted the bed-skirt, little dust bunnies fluttered through the air and I coughed.

"You okay Miss Harper?" Ella Mae called up. Man, how did she even hear me from down there?

"Yes ma'am," I said back. It was still a struggle to raise my voice too much.

I lifted the bed-skirt again and peered under the bed. A sliver of light shone through from the other side and there, near the wall, I saw something. A small box, maybe?

In order to get to it, I had to practically crawl underneath the bed. If anyone had walked into the room, they would have only seen the bottom half of my body sticking out. I stretched my arm and reached forward, finally grasping the elusive object.

Not a box. A picture frame.

A small silver double frame with a hinge that let it open and close. I sat on the hard wood floor, covered in dust, and opened the frame. On one side, a young woman with long brown hair piled on top of her head in a complicated twist of knots and braids. It was an old picture. So old that the color had long faded into browns and tans. The woman looked vaguely familiar. But that was sort of impossible, wasn't it?

In the second frame was a much newer picture of a group of girls in cheerleading uniforms. The uniforms were different from the kind the cheerleaders wore now, but they were still the same blue and black Demon colors. I studied the faces of the girls, then gasped. The one in the middle – the tall girl with blonde wavy hair – was my mother.

I was sure of it.

My heartbeat raced. How was this possible? I couldn't wrap my mind around it. I stood and moved to the window, wanting to get a better look in the light.

"Harper?" Ella Mae's voice at the bottom of the stairs.

Shit. There was no clear and fast rule about coming into these deserted rooms, but intuition told me they wouldn't want me in here. Not if they knew this picture had been left behind.

I shoved the bulky frame into the waistband of my sweatpants and quickly made my way to the top of the stairs. "Yes?"

"Are you alright? I thought I heard you coughing. Do you need anything?"

I shook my head. "No, I'm fine. Just had an itch in my throat."

"You look a little bit flushed," she said. Her hand gripped the banister like she was about to come upstairs and check on me. But I didn't want her up here. I needed more time to look around. Plus, I didn't want her to find the picture frame.

"Really, I'm fine. I just heard you calling and ran out here too fast. I'll just go lay down for a bit."

She hesitated, then looked back toward the kitchen. No doubt she still had a lot of work to do before the others got home from school. "Alright. But you call down if you need anything."

"I will," I said.

Back in my own room, I sat on my bed and took out the small frame. Carefully, I took it apart, separating the black velvet backing from the frame. The pictures were stuck to the glass inside, so I had to be very gentle with them. After a little bit of prodding, they both finally came loose.

On the back of the first picture, I could barely make out the hand-written words. Probably a name and date, but it was too smudged and faded to see. The picture of the cheerleaders was much more clear. In neat print, it read: Daneka, Julie, Claire, Mazie, and Audrey. The date was almost exactly twenty years ago.

I turned it over in my hand and studied the faces again. A young black girl with a wide, shining smile. Sheriff Hollingsworth? Next to her was an Asian girl that looked exactly like Lark Chen. Her mother maybe? That would put her at about the right age. The other three girls looked similar. White girls with blonde hair of varying lengths. But I knew the girl in the middle. Her smile beamed up at me from the photograph like a greeting from the grave.

Claire.

Knowing her name made my heart long for her.

But how was this possible? My mother had lived here in Peachville? Even if I believed in coincidence, this was way beyond that. What were the chances of me finding a picture of my mother here in a group home in Peachville, Georgia?

My gut told me it had nothing at all to do with chance.

NOT ANYMORE

THE FOLLOWING MORNING, Ella Mae pronounced me well enough to go back to school. To tell the truth, I was dreading it. Even though being at home had been kind of boring, I had no idea what to expect from the people at school. Agnes told me that no one believed I was responsible for what happened to Tori, which was a relief. But at the same time, everyone knew I had been questioned. So far, Tori's killer was still out there, and some people were bound to suspect me just because I'd been brought in.

Something tugged at the back of mind. Why had they brought me in for questioning? There had to be something linking me to the crime, but I couldn't for the life of me remember what. When I asked Ella Mae about it, she said the fever must have caused some temporary memory loss. Apparently, the doctor told her it was a possible side effect. The trouble was – I didn't remember seeing any doctors.

I hated this feeling of constant forgetfulness. I had an idea about my life since I first came to Shadowford, but when I tried to recall conversations and specific events, everything got confusing.

"You coming?"

Agnes stood outside the Shadowford van and waved me out. The ride to school had seemed short. My mind must have been wandering again. I was doing that a lot lately.

I walked toward the school with Agnes, pausing only for a moment to look up at the large stone demon statue. I remembered passing out by the statue my first day of school, and there was more, wasn't there? Some other connection to this statue I couldn't quite place.

"Are you sure you're okay to be back already?" Agnes said. "You seem kinda out of it."

I shook my head slightly. "I'm fine. Just having a hard time remembering stuff, you know?"

"Well, hopefully you'll remember all the stuff you learned before you were out sick. I think you've got a calculus test today."

I groaned and followed Agnes into the building.

For the most part, people were more polite than I expected. Sure, there were the whispers and some extra long glances my direction, but no one yelled at me or called me a murderer or anything obvious. The part of the day I'd been dreading, however, was lunch. When the lunch bell rang, I felt a twist in my stomach.

The cheerleaders. I didn't want to face them. What if they all blamed me for what happened to Tori?

I went through the line, then took the empty seat next to Agnes. I barely listened to the conversation around me, keeping my eye on the center table. I knew when they'd arrived. Everyone at the table turned to look, their stares lingering for a moment longer than you'd expect. That was the way it was with everyone when the cheerleaders walked into a room. It was like you couldn't take your eyes off them.

I set my burger down on the plate untouched. I couldn't eat anything. My stomach was in knots. I risked a look back and

saw the three friends walking together toward their table.
Brooke stopped mid-stride and looked straight at me. My
mouth opened and I sucked in a gulp of air. I wanted to look
away, but I froze instead.

Brooke turned to Lark and whispered something in her ear.
Lark glanced my way, then motioned to Allison. All three of
them were staring straight at me. I forced my gaze away.

"Oh my God, they're coming over," Agnes whispered.

My eyes widened and all my muscles tensed.

"Harper Madison," Brooke said. She was standing near my
chair. So close the edge of her sweater brushed against my arm.

"Yes?" I took a deep breath and waited for the insults. The
anger. The accusations.

"We need to talk," Lark said. To my surprise, she reached
over and grabbed my lunch tray. She started walking toward the
center table with her friends, then turned back to me. "Come
on."

I shared a confused look with Agnes, then shrugged. "I
guess I'll be back," I told her.

Agnes looked from me to the group of cheerleaders. "Fine,"
she said, crossing her arms in front of her. "Just go."

Was she mad at me? Did she think they were asking me over
there so they could be my friends? No way! These people were
probably going to filet me and eat me for lunch. I started to
explain it to her, but she had already turned away from me.
Screw it. I had enough to worry about.

I grabbed my backpack and headed over to the popular
table. Drake and Foster were already sitting down. I glanced at
Drake, expecting him to ignore me as usual, but instead he
stood up and pulled out a chair for me.

"Thanks," I muttered. Maybe he was building me up so he
could knock me down again. I sat.

Lark put my tray down and smiled. "You know, you don't
have to eat this crap if you don't want to."

Small talk? I was so confused. "I don't really like to get up early and make my own lunch," I said. "It's easier to just get food here I guess."

"I just mean that if you wanted, I could have my cook make something for you too," she said.

"Her mom's got a private chef at the mayor's mansion," Allison said. "The food is amazing."

Had I accidentally stepped through some portal to an alternate dimension? What was going on here?

Another boy from the football team came over carrying a bunch of paper bags. "Hey," he said. He smiled at me, then pulled out a plastic container. "Who had the turkey?"

"Me," Allison said, reaching for it. "Harper, have you met the boys? This is Jerry. Then Foster there in the white shirt. And Drake in the blue."

"She knows me," Drake said. He raised his eyebrows at me, then smiled.

I half smiled, confused as hell. I wondered if they were working to make me feel comfortable so they could later embarrass me in front of everyone or what?

Jerry passed out the rest of the food and everyone sat down to eat.

"So Harper, we heard you've been real sick," Brooke said. "How's your first day back at school?"

"We're so psyched to have you back," Lark said. "My mom was telling me about the whole interview thing at the police station. I can't imagine how horrible that must have been for you. She was so angry the police brought you in like that."

What whole interview thing? I didn't want to admit I had no idea what she was talking about.

"Yeah, that was crazy," Brooke said. "Everyone knows you barely even knew Tori. Why would you know anything about what happened to her?"

"Exactly," Allison said. "Totally ridiculous."

SARRA CANNON

I had no idea how to respond, so I sat quietly.

"What are your plans for this weekend, Harper?" Brooke looked at me expectantly.

The question threw me a bit. Why did she care? "I guess I'm just hanging around Shadowford as usual," I said. "Nothing too exciting."

"Are you planning to go to the game?" Drake asked.

"I guess. I think Shadowford girls always go." When I first came to PHS, the people at this table were making fun of me for being a so-called 'Shadowford freak'. Now, however, they let the reference pass by without comment, as if it didn't bother them at all.

"Sweet," Lark said. "But don't sit with those girls, okay? Come up and sit in our section."

I nearly choked on my water. "Why are you guys being so nice to me?"

The table grew quiet and everyone stared at me like they had no idea what I was talking about.

"Why wouldn't we be nice?"

"Just a few weeks ago you were making fun of me right here at this table," I said. I couldn't take it anymore. Being silent just wasn't my style. I had to know the truth. "So why are you being nice to me now? Because if you're just waiting for the right opportunity to make a fool out of me, I can just walk away right now."

I sounded a lot angrier than I intended. On the table, my fork rattled slightly on my tray. I slammed my hand over it to still the sound.

Lark was the first to speak. "I know we were totally rude that first week you were here. Tori could be kind of, well, bossy. She was upset with you over that whole ketchup incident. But now that Tori's gone, we all realize just how important it is to make up for the mistakes we've made."

104

So that's all I was to them? A mistake they'd made? And why weren't they more upset about Tori's death? They were acting like it was ancient history. I didn't know what kind of games they were playing, but I didn't want any part of it. I stood up, practically knocking my chair over backward.

"I need to get to class," I said. "Thanks for the offer, but I'll just sit with Agnes tomorrow at the game if I decide to go."

I took off before they had a chance to say anything else. Being nice to me was just their way of clearing their group conscience for being mean to me that first week, but how long was it really going to last? A couple of days? Then I'd go back to being the Shadowford reject that didn't deserve the time of day from any of them. Well, I didn't feel like being their little project of the week.

"Harper, hold up."

I turned to see Drake striding toward me. I stood in the doorway and when he caught up to me, I stepped through to the courtyard. He walked beside me as I headed toward my next class.

"What happened back there? I thought you'd be happy," he said.

"Happy that you guys are showing me charity?" I asked. "No thanks."

"Whoa, what makes you think it's charity? I think things got off on the wrong foot between us, that's all. We were all hoping to make some changes. You know, extend the invitation for you to hang out or something."

I stopped and turned to him. "You have to try to understand where I'm coming from here, Drake. You guys were all really mean to me my first week here. Then I get practically arrested and can't even remember why. And now, after being out sick with a terrible fever for a full week, I come back to find that you all are acting completely different toward me. How am I supposed to react? Eternally grateful that you're all descending from your thrones long enough to converse with a low-life like me?"

He put his palm on my cheek. I backed away, surprised, but he stepped forward and ran his fingertip along my chin line. "I was a real jerk to treat you like that," he said softly. "I understand if you want nothing to do with me, but I'm willing to do anything it takes to convince you that I'm sincere."

I swallowed hard. Was I overreacting?

"That first day we met in my sister's store, I thought you were beautiful," he said. He took my hand in his and caressed the side of my index finger with his thumb. "I was wrong to judge you for where you lived. But I don't care about any of that anymore. After Tori died, we realized that life's too precious to judge people on stupid things like where they live or who their parents are. We all really felt bad about how we treated you. But it's more than that."

"What do you mean?" My face tingled where his finger had been.

"There's just something about you," he said. "You're different from everyone else. We all can feel it. You're special, Harper."

Did he mean that? No one had ever spoken to me so warmly. It made my insides flutter.

"Harper?" I turned to see who had called my name. A guy with the clearest green eyes and brown, spiky hair was staring at me and Drake. I felt that familiar tickle at the back of my brain. I knew this guy from somewhere, but I couldn't remember his name.

"What do you want Jackson?" Drake asked.

"I wasn't talking to you Ashworth."

Jackson. It didn't ring a bell, yet he obviously knew who I was. "Do I know you?" I asked.

His face went pale. He looked from me to Drake and back again. His gaze went distant for a moment and his shoulders slumped slightly.

"Not really," he said. "Not anymore."

A sadness came over me that I didn't quite understand. Something in that guy's eyes had seemed so familiar. Like I'd known him in another life.

"Loser," Drake mumbled, then turned his attention back to me. "So what do you say? Please come to the game and sit in the reserved section? Then come out with us after the game?"

What the hell? I nodded. "Sure," I said. "Why not?"

I suddenly felt as though I had nothing more to lose.

A BETTER LIFE

I SPENT THE REST of the week sitting with Drake and the popular kids at lunch. At first, I felt awkward hanging out with Drake, knowing he used to date Allison. I didn't want to do anything that might make any of them upset with me. But when I asked Lark about it one day after lunch, she said that Allison didn't care at all. She said Drake and Allison were really just friends.

In the mornings, Allison, Brooke, and Lark had started waiting for me by the statue. It was like I had just slipped into their crowd and was now an accepted part of the group. And Lark was right, there was never any weird tension between Allison and me about Drake. I started to relax into my new friendships.

Agnes didn't seem to be too happy about my new friends. I told her she was welcome to hang out with us, but she said she wouldn't feel comfortable. When I mentioned it to Brooke, she scrunched up her nose.

"No offense," she said. "But Agnes is kind of a pain in the you-know-what."

"No she isn't. She's really nice. She was the first friend I made here in Peachville."

"I think she's nice too," Lark said. "But the problem is that she never stops talking. It's like blah-blah-blah all the dang time."

"It gets kind of old," Allison said.

I couldn't really argue with that, but I liked Agnes. She'd always been so nice to me. Well, except the past few days, I guess.

"Besides, you can hang out with Agnes anytime," Brooke said. "But I just don't think she'd really fit in with us."

I wondered if this had anything to do with Shadowford, but I guess if they really did have something against the place, they wouldn't have changed their minds about me. I still had no idea what made them want to be my friend, but it was nice to be part of a group for once. I'd changed schools so often that I'd pretty much always been on the outside. Being part of the popular crowd was a whole new experience for me.

In class, it even seemed like the teachers were nicer to me. A few of my teachers even gave me extra time on projects and tests. Mrs. King was especially generous, letting me skip a paper on Hemingway.

"I've seen your transcripts," she said. "You're way ahead of most of the rest of the students in your reading."

"Thanks," I said. "I could really use the extra time. I was a little behind after being out so long." That wasn't totally true. School out here in the sticks was way easier than some of the schools up in Atlanta. But at the same time, I did have a lot of homework to catch up on.

"Have you ever thought about trying out for the team?" she asked.

At first, I had no idea what she'd been talking about. "The team?"

"The cheerleading squad. Unfortunately, we've got an empty spot now that Tori's gone, and I'd really like to fill it with another sophomore. We're having tryouts next week if you're interested."

A strange shiver ran down my spine. I had never really considered trying out for a team sport or anything before. To be honest, I never stayed at one school long enough to really get involved. Then I thought of the picture I'd found of my mother. She had been a cheerleader here at this school twenty years ago. Maybe it was fate. Besides, I'd been feeling off ever since I got sick. I needed something to pull me back into the moment. "That might be fun," I said.

When I told the other girls about it at lunch, they freaked out.

"Oh my God! That's the best idea ever!" Lark said. She got up out of her chair and crossed over to give me a big hug. "I know you'd make the team, too. You've just got the look."

"I've never done anything like it before, though. I'm totally clumsy and uncoordinated sometimes. What if I can't learn the cheers fast enough?"

"We'll help you," Brooke said. "If she's looking for a sophomore to fill the spot, then you won't have too much competition anyway."

Competition. I suddenly thought of Agnes and how badly she wanted to be on the team. A knot of guilt formed in my stomach. I couldn't really back out now, though. I'd already told Mrs. King I would try out.

"After the game on Friday night, we should totally have a sleepover," Lark said.

"Ooh, we can teach you the cheers," Allison said, clapping. "Then you'll be way ahead of the other girls before practice even starts on Monday."

"We can have it at my house," Brooke said. "My parents won't mind at all."

"Is this a girls only party or are guys invited too?" Drake asked. He poked Foster in the ribs and they laughed.

Brooke rolled her eyes. "Duh. Girls only. But nice try."

"I was planning on throwing a party out at the lake house after the game," Foster said. "But it won't be any fun if you ladies can't be there."

"Do it next weekend," Lark said. "We can celebrate Harper making the squad."

Foster considered it. "Alright, that works. It's another home game," he said. "So party at the lake next Friday after the game. I expect all of you to be there."

I studied him. Foster had been dating Tori for over a year, yet here he was just a few weeks after she'd been brutally murdered, throwing a party for his friends like nothing happened. It was as though she were a part of their lives one day, and the next she was gone, and it was no big deal. They were all just moving on with their lives. It was weird.

Drake caught my eye and winked. I bit my lip and looked away, my face flushed with warmth. I couldn't believe that the most popular guy in school, the quarterback of the football team and son of one of the richest families in town, was flirting with me. It was like I had been reborn while I was sick and a new life had been given to me. A better life.

Tori's life.

I shook the thought away. No, this wasn't about Tori.

FRIDAY AFTERNOON CAME fast. As I was contemplating putting a temporary demon tattoo on my cheek for the game, something caught my eye out by the barn. Jackson Hunt was down there watching me through the window.

It wasn't the first time I'd seen him staring at me, either. After that first day in the courtyard when he interrupted me and Drake, I'd seen him watching me a lot. Both at school and here at Shadowford. Looking down at him now, I suddenly had a flash of memory. I'd seen him down there that first day I moved to Shadowford. Agnes had told me he was trouble and that we weren't supposed to be talking to him.

He waved up at me, but I didn't wave back. There was something so sad about him. It clouded my new happiness and brought back that same fuzziness that I'd felt when I first came out of the fever. I didn't like feeling like that. I wanted to be happy. I liked my new friendships even if I didn't totally understand why I had them.

I turned away from the window and walked into the bathroom to put the demon on my face.

I MUST HAVE SEEN
IT WRONG

*A*T THE GAME, Agnes asked me where I wanted to sit. She'd barely even talked to me the whole week, and I was surprised she even cared where I was sitting. Still, I hated to admit I'd been invited to the reserved section.

"Of course," she said. "Next thing I know, you'll be showing up at the tryouts next week to audition for the squad." There was so much bitterness in her voice.

I couldn't look her in the eye. "Agnes..." I'd been trying to figure out how to break the news to her, and now that the time had come, I wasn't sure what to say. Guilt twisted my stomach. Was I wrong to want something better for myself?

"You've got to be kidding me." She looked at me as if I'd just slapped her across the face. "I didn't think you'd actually do it. You know how much this means to me, Harper. And since when do you want to be a cheerleader? When you moved here, what was it you said about them? That they were ego-maniac airheads? My, my how things have changed."

"Agnes," I said. "Don't be upset. I'm sorry. It's not like I expected things to turn out like this. But-"

"But what? You're going to stab me in the back anyway?" Tears formed in her eyes. "Come on Courtney, let's go. We're not good enough to sit in the reserved section with Harper."

Courtney shrugged apologetically and gave me a little wave.

I felt like a real jerk. I knew how important the squad was to Agnes, but at the same time, didn't I deserve to be happy too? Never in my life had a group of people invited me into their circle the way the cheerleaders had. It was the first time I felt special, and I didn't want to give it up for anyone.

I made my way through the crowd to the small reserved section of bleachers just in front of where the cheerleaders stood. Mrs. King was already there and she smiled brightly when she saw me.

"Harper, I'm so glad you made it," she said. "Brooke told me you girls are going to her house to practice tonight, and I think that's such a great idea. Some of the other girls trying out were there for the auditions last year, so a lot of them will already be familiar with the cheers and the dances. It's really sweet that the girls are spending so much time with you. Friendship on the squad is so important, and even though we want to pick the best girls for the team, it doesn't hurt that you already get along with them so well."

I smiled. "I really feel lucky to be included," I said.

The game was much more exciting than the first one I'd gone to. I tried to pay special attention to all the cheers, but the thought of having to learn everything in just one week made me nervous. Plus, I couldn't help watching for Drake out on the field. He was really a star out there on the field. A couple of times when the defense was out on the field, I caught Drake watching me from the sidelines.

Everything was going great until the pyramid incident.

Sometime near the end of the third quarter, the cheerleaders did a cheer that had them piling up into a giant pyramid. A small brunette climbed to the top and stood, then with a little bounce, she was thrown high into the air. It was a beautiful stunt at first. She did a full flip in the air, but something went wrong on the landing. Her foot got caught on someone's arm and I gasped as she fell to the ground. Sitting so close to the squad, I had a clear view of the entire stunt. The girl's fall happened so fast. I jumped up, helpless to stop her. I could swear I heard a crack as her head hit the ground.

I screamed and jumped from my seat. The crowd around me gasped, then went silent. Mrs. King rushed out to where the other girls had huddled around the injured girl. I looked around, waiting for the paramedics to rush over, but I didn't see them.

My pulse hammered in my veins. She had to be hurt really bad. Possibly paralyzed. I watched as Mrs. King emerged from the huddle. She was smiling.

The small brunette stood up and waved to the crowd. Applause broke out all around me, but I stood there, stunned. How could that be possible? She had fallen at least ten feet straight down on her head. There was no way she was fine.

"Sherry never misses that toss," Mrs. King said. "Good thing Ella broke her fall."

I shook my head. "Are you sure she's alright? I could have sworn-"

"Goodness Harper, don't worry so much." Mrs. King laughed like it was nothing. "She's fine. In fact, I'm almost more worried about Ella's leg. Sherry practically fell right on top of it."

"I guess I must have seen it wrong," I said. But to be honest, I didn't think I had.

IT'S NOT THAT SIMPLE

*P*EACHVILLE WON THE game 21-7. Lark ran up to me in the bleachers, grabbed me by the arm, and pulled me out onto the field with her and the rest of the squad.

"You should go say hi to Drake," she said with a giggle. "He's so into you."

I blushed. "You really think so?"

"Duh. Don't even try to pretend you don't know he likes you," she said, then pushed me toward him on the field.

"Harper!" Drake called. He grabbed me up in a big bear hug and lifted me several inches off the ground.

I laughed harder than I remembered laughing in a very long time. "You were great," I said when he finally put me down.

"That's because I had the prettiest girl in the whole school right there, front and center," he said. "I wanted to impress you."

Me? The prettiest girl in school? Something about this felt so fake, but there was a part of me that wanted to believe it could be real.

"Have fun tonight," he said. He leaned down and kissed the top of my head, then ran off to join the rest of the team.

Afterward, at Brooke's, the girls drilled me about my relationship with Drake. We had all changed into cheer shorts and tank tops and were hanging out in Brooke's living room. The place was unreal. Sure, Shadowford was big, but this place was fancy. Plush carpeting. A huge stone fireplace. High ceilings. I was scared to touch anything.

"Has he asked you out yet?" Allison asked.

I searched her face to make sure there was no sign of jealousy about me dating her ex. She didn't ever talk about him, and now it seemed like she was encouraging me to date him. It was odd, but at the same time, I was glad I had the go-ahead to date him if he asked.

"No. He just mentioned that he hoped I'd be at the party next weekend."

"That's pretty much the same thing as a date, then," Lark said.

"I bet he's going to kiss you," Brooke chimed in.

"He practically kissed her tonight. Did you see him kiss her head? It was so sweet," Lark said.

"Stop," I said, hiding my head under a large velvet pillow. "You guys are embarrassing me."

"Harper's got a boyfriend," Allison sang.

"Oh Lord, what are you? Ten?" Brooke threw a pillow at Allison and she kicked back. Soon everyone was giggling and play-fighting, tossing pillows around the room and being silly.

I hid behind the couch, but Lark came around and started tickling me. We rolled on the floor and her shirt came up slightly, revealing a strange tattoo in the small of her back.

"What's that?" I asked, out of breath.

"What?" she asked, quickly pulling down her shirt.

"That tattoo?"

The room grew oddly quiet. Lark and Brooke exchanged glances. "I don't have a tattoo," she said, laughing. But her laugh came out nervous. She was hiding something.

"Yes you do," I said. "I saw it. Here, lift up your shirt."

"Stop," she said, moving away.

Her tone stung.

"Sorry," I mumbled. I hadn't meant to make anyone upset, but I had definitely seen something tattooed on her back. An animal of some sort, I thought. But there was a strangeness to it. The colors had been too bright. Maybe it was just one of those fake tattoos, and I had embarrassed her or something.

"Let's get to work," Brooke said.

Everyone gathered together in the middle of the room to teach me the cheers and after just a few minutes, the awkwardness of the tattoo incident was gone. But in the back of my mind, the oddness of it lingered. Between the girl who had fallen from the pyramid and now the weirdness of the tattoo, I felt like someone was keeping secrets from me.

At the same time, what did it matter? Was I willing to let a few secrets or awkward misunderstandings get in the way of my new happiness? No way. I threw myself into learning the cheers and the one dance the girls said would be used for the auditions next Thursday after school.

It took some serious work. I wasn't the most coordinated person in the world. But after a few times through, I was really getting the hang of it.

"Not bad," Brooke said. She gave me some pointers, then stood back to watch me run through the cheers one more time. "If you keep working hard this week, I don't see any reason you wouldn't make the squad."

"Really?" Thinking about the auditions made me nervous. I didn't even want to see who all showed up Monday.

"You've got this," Lark said, squeezing my arm.

I smiled, feeling better now that she seemed to have forgiven me for the whole tattoo thing. "I'm going to run to the bathroom," I said. Brooke told me where I could find one and I rushed out of the room.

When I came back, though, I heard them talking about me. I pressed against the wall, staying out of sight.

"Why can't we tell her, though?" That was Allison. "If she's the Prima, why can't we just tell her everything and get it over with?"

"It's not that simple," Lark said.

"You need to be more careful about who sees that tattoo," Brooke said.

So I was right about her having one, but why did it matter? It wasn't like I was going to judge anyone for having a dumb tattoo.

"I know. I didn't mean to show it, but we were playing around and my shirt came up. It happens."

I scooted closer to the edge of the wall, hoping to hear better, but my toe made a popping sound. I cringed as the living room went silent.

"Harper?"

I tiptoed back down the hall a bit, then walked normal, as if I was just coming back. "Yep," I said. "What's next on the agenda?"

"Sleep," Brooke said with a yawn. "It's already almost three-thirty."

Later, after everyone had climbed into sleeping bags on the living room floor, my mind refused to rest. Everything had been so strange since my illness, and things just weren't adding up. Allison had said I was the Prima. What did that mean exactly?

Fragments of a strange dream I'd had when I was passed out with fever came to me suddenly. A silver knife. A woman with blood red eyes.

"The Prima has finally come home," the voice had said in my dream.

I felt along the diagonal scar on my palm. Ella Mae had told me I cut my hand on a piece of glass when I passed out in the bathroom that night after I got back from the police station. She said I'd been holding a cup of tea and when I fell, it broke.

One of the jagged pieces sliced open my hand. I'd believed her.
But now...

I wasn't so sure.

PROMISE ME

*T*HE DAY AFTER the slumber party, I stood by my bedroom window for a long time. Waiting.

Around two in the afternoon, I saw him. Jackson came around the side of the barn and slipped inside. I needed to talk to him. I forced myself to walk normal all the way through the hall, down the stairs and out the back door. I glanced around the yard to make sure no one was watching, then hurried in after him.

"What are you doing here?" he asked. He was sitting on a crate near the back of the barn, smoking a cigarette, and I felt the strongest wave of deja vu.

"Looking for you," I said.

"Ah." He slid off the top of the crate and came toward me. "This is a first, but I'll go with it."

"What do you mean?"

"I mean I've been here before," he said.

I studied him. I didn't think he was talking about deja vu, but it was strange that I had just had that feeling of having been here before too.

"If you've been here before, then how is this a first?"

"It's hard to explain," he said. "Besides, you'd probably just forget even if I told you."

My stomach tightened. "What do you know about me forgetting things?"

He sighed and shook his head. "Nothing, Harper. It doesn't matter."

"It matters to me," I said. "Ever since I got sick, I've been having these weird moments where I feel like I'm almost remembering something that happened to me. Then, I lose it. Like I'm not sure what's real and what was a dream."

That same sad look crossed his face again. "I can't help you," he said. "It's too late."

"Too late? What are you talking about?"

"I'm talking about this." He picked up my scarred hand and opened it, palm up.

"Your mother told me I fell and cut my hand on a teacup."

He snorted. "Don't believe everything you hear."

"I keep remembering this crazy dream. There were these people chanting all around me and a woman with red eyes cut me with a silver knife. She called me the Prima."

Jackson's eyes grew wide and he tilted his head to the side. "The Prima?"

I nodded.

"Are you sure that's what she said?"

"I'm not sure of anything," I said. "So many things are fuzzy. Like you. That day in the courtyard when I came back to school. You acted like we knew each other, but I couldn't remember ever talking to you before. What does it mean, anyway?"

"I can't talk to you about this," he said, throwing his cigarette to the ground and stomping on it. He started to walk toward the door, but I stepped into his path.

"Why not?"

"There are rules, Harper. I know you don't understand what's going on here, but I'm bound by an oath older than time."

Deja vu again. I'd heard those words before, I was certain.

"There are rules I have to follow."

"Whose rules?"

He shook his head. "I can't tell you."

"But something is strange about this place. I can feel it." I paced in front of the door. "Were you at the game last night? One of the cheerleaders broke her neck when she fell off the top of the pyramid. I heard it. But she got up and she was fine. Like nothing ever happened. But I know what I saw. I feel like I'm going crazy."

Jackson ran a hand through his hair. "I wish I could help you. I tried," he said. "But you've got a new life now, am I right?"

"I don't know," I said. "Sometimes I feel happier than I've ever felt before, but then other times, it feels like everyone is lying to me."

"I've gotta go." He moved around me and pushed open the door, but I grabbed his hand and pulled him back.

"Please," I said. "What is a Prima?"

He looked deep into my eyes and I knew that we were connected somehow. I couldn't explain it. Slowly, he leaned down and took my head in his hands. He was going to kiss me, and in that moment, I wanted him to. I leaned forward and our lips met.

A flash of memory jolted through me. I was in his room and we were kissing. Everything we'd talked about and been through came back to me in a heady rush. The drawings. The room full of flames. I pulled away, gasping. Tears sprang to my eyes.

"What happened?" I asked. "Why couldn't I remember?"

"Listen to me," he said. "You're going to forget again. Soon. It's part of the spell. But you can fight it, Harper. From the moment I saw you, I knew you were different from the other girls."

His words were almost the same as what Drake had said to me. I opened my mouth to ask him what made me so different from everyone else, but he placed a finger over my lips.

"We don't have much time," he said. "Do you remember the drawing? The one of you standing in a room of flames?"

I remembered.

"I think it's going to happen soon. I drew it again last night, but this time the picture was different," he said. He ran his hand along my collarbone and fingered the sapphire pendant around my neck. "This time you were wearing your necklace. Promise me you won't take it off, okay? Promise you'll wear it every single day, no matter what."

I nodded.

Jackson leaned down and brushed my lips lightly with his, then slid out of the barn. No matter how hard I tried to hold onto them, moments later my memories of him began to fade.

THIS WEEK IS GOING TO BE TOUGH

*M*ONDAY AFTERNOON, I joined eight other sophomore girls in the gym for cheerleading tryouts. Never in my life had I even considered being friends with a cheerleader, much less actually trying to become one. Until Peachville. Everything was different here. Ever since I lost my adoptive family and was put into the foster care system, I'd been looking for a place where I could fit in. All I ever wanted was to belong somewhere. To have a family who truly cared about me and wanted me in their lives. From the way Brooke and the others interacted, they seemed like a family. And if I could become a part of that, it might be the closest I'd ever come to my dream. At least while I was still in high school.

If I didn't make the squad, I wasn't sure what would happen to my friendship with the other girls. They had become my friends before Mrs. King ever mentioned the tryouts, so I wanted to believe that win or lose, they would still be my friends. But at the same time, being a part of the team would mean daily practices, special trips, away games, and all kinds of time spent together. I wanted it bad.

When Agnes walked into the gym and saw me already sitting on the shiny floor with my loaner pom poms, my stomach tensed. A scowl crossed her face and she took a deep breath, then shaking it off, she smiled and walked straight over to me.

"Hey," she said, grabbing some blue pom poms from the pile and sitting down next to me. "Look, I know I've been really weird about this whole cheerleading thing. But I don't like not being able to be friends with you. And I know I can't expect you not to make friends here at PHS or want to be a part of such an awesome squad. Besides, I was thinking that it would suck if we were mad at each other over this forever. One of us might make the squad now and the other one might audition for next year's squad."

"I guess that's true," I said. I hadn't thought about next year's auditions yet. I wasn't in the habit of thinking so far ahead at a new school. "I'm glad you came over to talk to me. I hate not being able to talk to you like we used to."

"I know, me too." Her smile seemed genuine. "Let's just try to forget about any kind of jealousy and try to have fun this week."

"Sounds good to me," I said.

Mrs. King walked through the door and clapped a few times. "Girls, I'm so happy you all came out today. We never anticipate having to replace a member of our squad like this, and what happened is a terrible tragedy for our entire school. At the same time, I know Tori would have wanted us to move on and compete in the state cheerleading competitions this winter and next spring. In order to do that, we have to have one more girl, so that's why we're all here today.

"As you know, I've only asked sophomores to come out today. That's because I want to keep the current squad balanced and make sure there are enough experienced members to move up next year. With that said, this week is going to be tough. I expect you to be here every afternoon this week from three to five. If you are late, you'll be automatically disqualified. Any questions?"

Agnes raised her hand.

"Yes, Agnes?"

"I was wondering if there are any extra rehearsals planned for those of us who want to put in more time and make sure we've really got them down?"

"As a matter of fact, there will be an extended practice at my house on Wednesday afternoon with the current squad. All of you are invited to attend, but it's not mandatory. It will be a good opportunity to spend time with the squad and see how you fit in and to watch the more experienced girls do the routines," she said. "That will be from five to six-thirty or so."

She glanced around the room. No one else had any questions.

"Let's get started, then."

For the next two hours, Mrs. King and some of the other cheerleaders took us through the routines and cheers I learned Friday night. Some of these girls were serious competition. Including Agnes. She obviously knew her stuff.

I didn't do too badly, but I was still struggling with a few of the routines, especially the long dance.

"Don't worry," Agnes said after practice while we were waiting for Ella Mae to pick us up. "You'll get the hang of it. It's the same dance we learned at last year's tryouts, so I already knew it, but you've almost got it down already. If you want to practice some at home this week, just come and get me."

"Thanks. I'm really glad we're talking again. I would hate to lose you as a friend."

"I know, me too." She looked at me with a smile, then her eyes traveled down toward my neck and her face fell. Confusion flashed across her features.

I touched my pendant self-consciously. "What's wrong?"

She shook her head slightly. "Nothing," she said. "I thought you lost that."

"What? My pendant?" I looked toward the ground, trying to remember. "I don't think so."

A distant memory threatened to rise to the surface, but was lost in a sea of mist. The cut on my hand began to throb.

IS THIS SUPPOSED TO BE A GOOD LUCK CHARM?

*B*Y THE TIME Wednesday's practice arrived, I felt much more confident about the routines. I felt like I was finally settling in somewhere for the first time. It was nice to have friends and make plans for the future. At lunch, I always sat with Brooke and the others. Drake had started walking me to my classes. Nothing old fashioned like offering to carry my books or anything, but he was obviously paying a lot of attention to me.

I wondered if any of that would change if I didn't make the squad.

The idea of becoming a cheerleader was quickly becoming an obsession with me. I spent my evenings practicing the routines either with Agnes or on my own. Except for calculus, my school work was pretty easy. All I cared about was keeping these new friendships and making it into their elite group.

Wednesday, I felt nervous all day. This would be our last chance to practice the routines before the actual auditions on Thursday.

"Don't look so nervous," Brooke said as she walked me to the gym. "It'll show on your face. Just keep your smile turned on at all times and you'll be fine."

"I hope so," I said. But now, I felt nervous about being too nervous. Ugh.

"You've got this in the bag for sure," Lark said.

"You haven't even watched us practice yet," I said.

"Eh, I just have a feeling about you." She winked at me and linked her arm in mine.

Why was everyone saying that lately? Before I moved to Peachville, every family I'd lived with had been dying to get rid of me as fast as possible. But here? People actually thought I was special.

She's the Prima.

A voice echoed in my head, and I stumbled.

"You okay?"

"Gosh, Harper. You better get it together by tomorrow. Clumsy up like that at auditions and you're toast."

"Brooke! Don't say something like that to her," Lark said in my defense. "You'll make her even more nervous than she already is."

I was disoriented and thankful to have Lark's arm to keep me steady as we walked. While in some ways, I had been happier than ever, I also knew that deep in my mind, there was a locked room of secrets I seemed to be keeping from myself. Like I had hidden information and memories away somehow. And every once in a while, like this voice, they would pop to the surface and scare the bejeesus out of me.

During practice in the gym, I was off the whole time. I tripped. I forgot the dance choreography. I even yelled out the wrong words on one of the cheers. Mrs. King eyed me suspiciously, but thankfully didn't call attention to my mistakes. I knew that if I didn't get it together, I wouldn't have a chance.

When the two hours were up, Mrs. King called us all together to wish us luck for the following day. "Everyone is invited to my house this afternoon, so carpool over together if you want."

I rode with Brooke, Lark and Allison in Brooke's BMW.

"Nice car," I said.

The sleek blue car was amazing. All leather interior. Sunroof. All the bells and whistles. I felt uncomfortable sitting in it, wondering how I was supposed to fit in with a group of girls like this. Rich girls. The mayor's daughter. The cream of the crop. Come to think of it, not one single girl on the cheerleading squad was poor like me. All of them had wealthy, successful parents. My gut churned.

I would never be able to match them in clothing and bags and cars. I would always be a hanger-on. Maybe I could get a job or something to help pay for some of the things they all seemed to have. I pushed it from my mind and tried to enjoy the ride.

"I can't wait for the party Friday night," Lark said. "This is definitely the week Andrew is going to kiss me."

"And Drake definitely has his eye on someone in this car," Allison teased. "Not going to name names." She pointed at me and everyone laughed.

"If I don't make the squad, I'm not too sure I'll feel like partying," I said. What I meant was that I wasn't sure I would still be invited.

"Oh pooh," Lark said. "You're going to make it."

The three girls exchanged glances. Brooke turned the wheel sharply and pulled over on the side of the road.

"Why are we stopping?" The abandoned parking lot we sat in front of was definitely not Mrs. King's house. I swallowed nervously. There was an excited energy in the car I couldn't quite put my finger on.

Brooke smiled and reached for something in the glove compartment.

"Harper, I have something for you," she said. A deep blue velvet jewelry box sat in her palm. She held it out to me. "Open it."

My hand shook a little as I took the box from her hand. It squeaked as I opened it. I gasped as I looked inside. A black diamond pendant as big as an acorn sat inside. It was strung onto a beautiful, delicate silver chain.

"Don't get too excited," Brooke said. "I'm not giving it to you to keep forever. But I want you to promise me you'll wear this to the audition tomorrow."

My hand instinctively rose up to my mother's sapphire pendant. "Why?"

She smiled and looked at me over her shoulder. "Actually, wear it for this run through at Mrs. King's house."

I ran my finger along the smooth surface of the stone. "Is this a real diamond?"

"Yes," she said. "It's extremely old and extremely powerful."

I'd never heard anyone refer to a diamond as powerful. The word sent a cold shiver down my spine. "What does it do?"

"You'll see," Lark said, raising her eyebrows.

Allison, who was sitting next to me in the backseat, reached around my neck and unclasped my mother's silver chain. My hand went to my throat.

"Wait," I said. "I never take that off."

"You can't wear them both," Allison said. "It won't work."

Work? What exactly was going on with this diamond? "Is this supposed to be a good luck charm or something?"

"Something like that," Brooke said. She took the black diamond necklace out of the box and put it around my neck.

Allison put my sapphire necklace into the box and I bit my lip nervously.

"We'll give it back to you tomorrow after the tryouts," Brooke said, seeing my concern. "I promise."

Brooke slipped the box into the glove compartment and closed it tight. I knew it was silly, but for some reason, I felt uneasy without it. Like taking it off meant letting someone down. But that was ridiculous right?

I glanced longingly at the glove compartment, then settled back into the leather seat, the cold weight of the diamond heavy against my skin.

A DEMON ON HIS BACK

RS. KING'S HOUSE was huge considering she and Coach King didn't have any children. They were barely out of college, really. As I looked up at the large brick house with its perfect yard and big bay windows, I wondered how two teachers could afford something so expensive. I dreamed that someday I could have something like this with a husband who loved me and a job I was good at.

Maybe I would settle down in Peachville someday. If Drake and I stayed together, we could certainly afford whatever kind of house we wanted. I mentally kicked myself for having thoughts like that. I wasn't even Drake's girlfriend yet and already I was planning our wedding and spending his family's millions. I had never thought of myself as that kind of girl. You know, the materialistic kind who liked people for their money. A pang of guilt shot through my body.

I guess that was just one of the side-effects of being friends with all these rich popular kids who had everything handed to them on a silver platter. It put my head in the clouds and made me feel like I was entitled to things I had no business daydreaming over.

In the backyard, the cheerleading squad assembled to run through the routines. All of the sophomore wannabes sat in the plush grass and watched. The sun faded in the evening sky and I had to put my jacket on to keep from shivering.

"Demons. Let's do it again. Fight. Demons fight!"

It amazed me how together they were. Completely synchronized down to every movement. Even if I made the team, how would I ever look as polished as they were?

When it came time for us to run through the dance with the squad, side-by-side, Mrs. King put me in the front next to Brooke. She was by far the best and most beautiful on the squad, so standing beside her made me super nervous. I fingered the black diamond under my shirt.

The music began and suddenly, I felt an energy buzz through my muscles. All of my nervousness left me and it was like instinct took over. I smiled bright, just like the girls had told me to, and ran through the routine flawlessly. Where I'd frozen earlier in practice, this time I didn't even have to think about the moves. It was like my body already knew it so well. I felt so incredibly coordinated and energetic. Strong and confident.

"Great job!" Mrs. King clapped her hands together, then stepped forward and whispered, "Especially you, Harper. That was awesome. Keep it up."

I felt giddy. High on raw energy and adrenaline. If Mrs. King had asked me to do a somersault back-handspring across her lawn, I could have done three of them in a row. Against my skin, the diamond was now so warm it almost burned.

When the squad started a new routine, I excused myself to go to the bathroom. I needed to catch my breath. The power in my veins was exhilarating, but it was also a little scary. I teetered on the edge of excitement and losing control. I knew what it was like to go over that edge and lose control. It always seemed to end with me being sent off to yet another foster home.

I opened the sliding glass door and stepped inside the warm living room. I heard voices in the next room and paused, not wanting to interrupt by passing through. Coach King stood in the middle of the kitchen with one of the cheerleaders. Ella, I think. Her brown hair was pulled into a loose ponytail and she was sitting on top of the granite counters, giggling. Coach King leaned in toward her and whispered something in her ear that made her squeal.

I backed up a step. I needed to go through the kitchen to get to the bathroom, but this was obviously something I wasn't supposed to see. Definitely not your average teacher-student relationship. As I backed up, I bumped into something and almost knocked it over. When I turned to catch it, I saw that it was a coat rack.

I gripped the round middle of it and steadied it, but one coat fell to the floor in a heap. I grimaced, then glanced to the kitchen. They hadn't heard me. Quietly, I leaned over to pick up the coat.

When my hand touched the leather sleeve, an image sliced through my mind, causing me to drop it suddenly. I closed my eyes and gripped my forehead. Where had that come from? I crouched down, knees bent as I tried to make sense of what I had seen. Another memory, I knew, but of what?

I touched the jacket again, this time turning it over in my hands so I could study it. It was a blue and black letterman's jacket. The kind the football players wore. There, stitched onto the back was the face of the Demon mascot.

The memory came to me full force. It was like being hit with lightning.

Searching for my lost necklace under the bleachers. Tori Fairchild with her long blonde hair and flirtatious laughter, standing on the field with a boy. No, someone older than us. A man in a football jacket and cap. He saw me. Threatened me.

Coach King? It couldn't have been! But here he was in his own kitchen, boldly flirting with a different cheerleader. He had been the one with Tori that night. I hadn't seen his face, but I saw the jacket. Drake's jacket didn't look like this. There was no Demon on the back. They must have changed the design of the jacket years ago, when Coach King was still a student.

"Harper?" Coach King stood behind me. My heart hammered against my ribs.

I took a deep breath and tried to steady my nerves. "Hey coach. Sorry, I accidentally knocked over the coat rack."

He looked from me to the football jacket in my hand. Could he see my fear? Did he know it was me that night under the bleachers? I'd been so sure that he never saw my face, but what if I was wrong?

"I thought I heard something in here," he said. "Here, let me get that for you." He took the jacket from my hand and put it back up on the rack. "Was there something else you needed?"

I stood there, unable to remember what I had even come in the house for in the first place. I shook my head. "No. I mean, yeah. Where's your bathroom?"

He hiked his thumb over his shoulder. "Back there, through the kitchen and down the hall. It'll be the first door on your right."

I thanked him and hurried down the hallway. In the bathroom, I splashed cold water on my face. Had Coach King killed Tori? A thousand possible scenarios flooded my mind. Maybe she threatened to break up with him. Or maybe he wanted to break it off with her and she threatened to tell.

My breath came in short, shallow gasps. The room seemed to be spinning.

They had seemed very happy together that night out at the football field. But what if I wasn't the only one who saw them there together?

My flesh broke out in goosebumps.

What if Mrs. King saw them? Wives were always going into murderous rages over their cheating husbands. If she found out her husband was cheating on her with one of her own students, she might have snapped and killed Tori.

She was burned alive. Cooked from the inside.

Sheriff Hollingsworth's words jumped into my mind. I had forgotten until now just how strange Tori's murder had really been. She was cooked alive. The Sheriff had accused me of it, saying that I had certain powers. She'd mentioned the fire that killed my adopted father. She'd known all along that someone like me had killed Tori.

Not Coach King. His wife!

I was kidding myself if I thought this town was normal. American as apple pie and all the bull. Deep down, I knew it was different. Was that why I fit in better here than anywhere else I'd ever lived? It was the real reason they wanted me to be a part of the cheerleading squad. To keep an eye on me. Because I was like them.

A witch.

That was what Jill, my adoptive mother had called me after the fire.

Someone knocked on the bathroom door and I jumped. My heart stopped beating for a second, then started back up again, going ninety miles an hour.

"Yes?" My voice cracked.

"Are you alright in there sweetheart?" It was Mrs. King. Did she know that I remembered? Was she the one responsible for Tori's death?

"I'll be out in a second," I choked out.

The picture I'd found in the empty bedroom came into my mind. My mother. Lark's mother, the mayor. Sheriff Hollingsworth. They were all there in the picture. Mrs. King was too young, but she had been a cheerleader when she was in school too.

The truth hit me like a ton of bricks, weighing down my chest and making my breathing labored. They were all witches. The whole town was full of them. I had spent my whole life denying what I really was, but now I knew.

"Are you sick?" She sounded concerned.

The black diamond burned my skin. I pulled it out of my shirt so that it was no longer touching my bare flesh. No wonder I had done so well on the rehearsal tonight. I wasn't high on adrenaline. I was high on magic.

Mrs. King knocked lightly on the door again. "Harper, honey?"

I needed to get back to my room and gather my thoughts. I pulled myself together as best I could and opened the door. "I think I might have pushed a little too hard tonight," I said. "I think I need to go home."

"I'll get Brooke to drive you and Agnes home, alright?" Her face was full of worry. I was just relieved she didn't look angry.

I waited out by the car until Brooke and Agnes appeared.

"What's wrong?" Brooke asked.

"Just think I've been working too hard," I lied.

Agnes looked disappointed to be leaving early, but she stayed quiet in the backseat on the way home. When we got to Shadowford, I reached into the glove compartment for the velvet box. I started to unclasp the black diamond, but Brooke stopped me.

"Keep it," she said after Agnes had gotten out of the car. "You'll wear it tomorrow and you'll do your very best. Do you understand?" Her tone was serious and cold. Threatening.

I nodded. I was in too deep to back out now.

I HAVE CARRIED
MY FEAR

*T*HAT NIGHT, I spent a lot of time alone in my room studying the pictures I had found. My coming to Peachville was no coincidence. But it couldn't have been entirely masterminded either. After all, wasn't it my own actions at the various foster homes that led me here? No, it was more like fate that brought me here to the town where my mother lived.

I had so many questions about her. Why did she give me up for adoption? How did she die? Was she different like me? Could she make things move with her mind when she got angry? In the photograph, she wore her long blonde hair in a ponytail high on her head. A blue ribbon was tied perfectly around it. She was smiling and beautiful, but there was also worry in her eyes.

I wished I could have known her. More than anything, I wanted to talk to her and have her explain this strange town to me. Were the women here witches? Or did they just have access to some kind of supernatural power?

I realized I was different at an early age. Ever since the night of the fire when I was eight years old. I knew. But I never knew there were others like me.

And now I had a chance to join them. Who knew what kind of power they had access to? Maybe they could even teach me how to control my power. So far, it only reared its ugly head when I was angry or extremely upset about something. And then, my emotions were usually so out of control, I ended up causing someone pain or destroying everything around me.

The fire was my fault, but I didn't mean to do it. I was just a little girl and my parents were fighting. Heath, my adoptive father, kept yelling at Jill and hitting her. I couldn't stand it. I went into the living room and watched them, tears streaming down my face. I remember how the anger and hurt inside of me boiled up so hot I could literally feel my temperature rise. I felt so helpless. So small. He slapped her again and I snapped. The anger consumed me. I remember feeling the wind in my hair and thinking a window must be open.

Then the wind grew stronger. More fierce. Suddenly, all of the objects in the room rose up. Vases, picture frames, anything that wasn't nailed down was floating in the air. A painting above the fireplace fell off the wall and clattered to the floor, then rose up again. A glass of wine on the mantle. A book sitting on the side table. A candle in the dining room. They all rose several inches into the air.

Heath looked at me in shock. His eyes filled with awe, then, slowly, disgust. He yelled curses at me, told me to stop. He said I was a witch. An evil child. He said they made a mistake adopting me. His words only confused me. I was scared by what was happening around me, and inside, my emotions were out of control. Anger, hurt, confusion. I felt all of those things.

When he came toward me, I panicked. I screamed and suddenly, the objects in the room flew in different directions, crashing wildly against the wall or the floor. I ran, but he followed. At some point, something must have flown into the fire that was burning in the fireplace. The fire marshal said the fire was spread around the room as though a tornado had come through there. It was my fault, but I never meant for anyone to get hurt.

I ran into my room and the door shut behind me without me even having to touch it with my hand. It was like it only happened because I wanted it to happen. Outside, I could hear Heath yelling for me to open the door. Within minutes, smoke began to pour into the room. In the distance, I heard Jill scream. Behind me, the window broke and a neighbor pulled me through. She saved my life and I didn't even know her name. Jill escaped out the back door, but Heath was trapped inside. He died in the fire and Jill never recovered. She didn't want to believe what I had done, but she saw it happen and could never reconcile it in her mind. She spent six years in a mental hospital, then committed suicide by taking a handful of pills one night. I have carried the guilt of that night on my shoulders for the past eight years.

I have also carried my fear. Fear of getting angry and causing something terrible to happen to someone else. Fear of never learning to control this strange power. Fear that no one would ever love me or understand me.

Here in Peachville, though, there were people who were just like me. They were asking me to join them. I knew they could teach me to control it and make sure that no one was ever hurt by my anger again.

They could help me.

But at what cost?

WE WERE CONNECTED SOMEHOW

A WOMAN IN WHITE came to me in my dreams that night. She was young and full of life. The sun followed her around and she walked in a garden of the most amazingly beautiful flowers. When she laughed, it sounded like happiness.

The woman sat by a fountain, and I recognized it. The fountain from the garden at Shadowford. Only clean and running with sparkling, cool water. She dipped her hand into the water and smiled.

But a cloud covered the sun and filled the garden with shadows. The woman looked up, fear written across her features. She stood, then ran to the house. In my dream, Shadowford Manor was different. Freshly painted, there were no vines crawling up the side and no creaking boards on the front porch. I thought this must be how it used to look a hundred and fifty years ago when it was new.

I followed the woman in white as she ran up the front steps and into the house. Darkness followed her, turning everything gray. I heard a loud crack as a bolt of lightning shot across the sky.

The woman ran up the stairs, looking behind her as though she were being followed. But she wasn't looking at me. It was more as though I were a ghost and she was merely looking through me.

When she turned her face, I saw that I knew this woman. She was the same woman from the photograph. The picture frame I'd found in the empty bedroom. I wondered who she was. I followed her up the stairs to the second floor, then down to the end of the hall, just past the last bedroom. At first, I thought she was trapped. There was nowhere else for her to run. But she placed her hand on a section of dark wood paneling in the wall and a door opened.

Stairs appeared in the opening. A secret passageway up to the third floor. The woman looked back one last time, terror on her face, then disappeared up the stairs. I tried to follow her, but as I stepped into the shadows, I lost my footing and fell. I fell through the house and down into darkness.

I sat up in bed, out of breath. Sweat trickled down my back. My bedroom was dark, but a sliver of moonlight shone through my window. The picture of the woman in white lay on my bedside table and I picked it up. It was definitely her, but who was she?

Somewhere in the house, I heard a scream. Distant, but real. I rushed out of bed and went to my door. When I turned the knob, the door was locked.

I ran to my desk, got the same bobby pin I'd used the night Tori died, and quickly unlocked the door. In the hallway, it was pitch dark. It took my eyes a few seconds to adjust, and then I could only make out the dark silhouettes of big objects like the grandfather clock on the landing. I tiptoed down the hall.

I wasn't sure where the scream had come from, but I had a feeling I now knew how to reach the third floor of the house.

Was that where they'd taken me when they cut my hand? I wondered.

I walked slowly to the end of the hall. My long nightshirt billowed around my legs and I shivered. I had no idea what I was getting myself into, but I wanted to know the truth. Whoever that woman was, she had lived in this house before. Maybe over a hundred years ago. And she wanted me to know how to get up to the third floor.

I felt along the wall until I was sure I was in the right place. In the darkness, I could make out the door to the empty bedroom at the end of the hall, and just past that, the wood paneling where the woman had opened the hidden staircase.

With a deep, ragged breath, I put my hand against the smooth wood surface and pushed. I gasped as the panel gave way and a door opened in front of me. A light from above spilled down and illuminated the stairs. They were narrow and worn. I stepped onto them with my bare feet and was surprised to find that they were strangely warm.

I hesitated before putting all of my weight on that first step, remembering my dream. But as I carefully moved forward, I realized that these stairs were solid. I climbed up, letting my hands run along the walls that framed either side of the strange staircase.

At the top, I half expected to find a coven of witches performing some strange ritual on a screaming girl. But there was no one. There was only a large circular room with a round table in the center. A red candle in the center of the table flickered, sending shadows across the room. Someone must have been there or the candle wouldn't be lit. I stepped fully into the room and took a better look around. That's when I noticed the doors. Five identical wooden doors spaced equally around the room. The door was open where I had come through, but all four of the others were closed.

I crossed to the closest door on my left. The door knob was black and smooth and when I touched it, I felt a heaviness in my stomach like a warning. I turned the knob and slowly opened the door. It creaked as it opened, and I winced at the loud sound, afraid someone might hear me.

Inside was a small library packed with books. A torch glowed on the wall, sending a warm amber light across the room. The ceiling was higher than I thought possible for the third floor of the house, but maybe it was a trick of the eye. Bookcases ran from floor to ceiling all around the room. I walked inside and glanced at the books. There were tomes of various sizes and shapes and colors. Some were ancient looking with cracked spines, while others were bound in materials I couldn't honestly identify. A lot of the titles were foreign, so I couldn't tell what they were about.

I randomly selected one book with a bright green binding from the shelf. The books were so jammed in there, I had to really pull to get it out, and when it did slide out, it was heavier than I thought it would be.

The words inside were handwritten, and when I looked closer, they looked more like symbols than words. Kind of like Chinese characters, but different. I ran my finger along a line of symbols, feeling how they were slightly upraised. The paper itself was ragged at the edges and bumpy, like it had been handmade a very long time ago.

I wedged the book back onto the shelf. I couldn't reach the upper shelves, but there was no ladder in the room, and I wondered how anyone got to them. I wanted to stay longer to see if I could find a book written in English, but I was afraid that if I stayed too long, someone would find me up there and I would be in some serious trouble.

I went back out to the main room, closing the door behind me. The next door down opened into another room of shelves. But this time, the shelves were full of jars and boxes. Spices, strange liquids, spiders, and all sorts of things I couldn't identify. Probably things like eye of newt and tail of rat, although mostly it just looked like herbs and such.

A table along the far wall was covered with small glass vials. *For making potions?*

I wondered what type of potions and elixirs a witch could make with all of these ingredients. Would I have the opportunity to learn how?

A tingle ran up my spine as I noticed a large painting of the woman from my dream. Her hair was up in braids and she was smiling. Below the frame, a brass plate said simply, "Prima." I shivered and ran my fingers across the carved wood of the frame. Whoever she was, we were connected somehow.

Behind the third door was a room with three metal bed-frames. The mattresses had been removed, but there were chains attached to the sides of the beds. It looked like a torture chamber or the kind of place they kept crazy people. I didn't like this room. It was cold and dark and had a strong metallic smell, like blood. I left quickly.

The fourth and final door was heavier than the others. It had the face of a demon carved into the wood. At first, I thought it was stuck, so I gave it a hard yank. It finally gave way when I put all of my weight behind it.

I peered inside.

Oh my god.

My hand flew to my mouth and I backed away, frightened. Through the door was a long hallway. Longer than was possible in a house this size. Doors stretched out as far as I could see before surrendering to the shadows. At least ten on each side that I could count from where I stood.

But how was that possible? The house wasn't big enough for there to be so many doors here at the top.

I must still be dreaming.

I rubbed my eyes, then looked again. This couldn't be explained by a trick of the light. There were too many doors. This had to be magic of some sort.

Slowly, I stepped across the threshold. A cool breeze began to blow toward me, lifting my hair off my neck. My mouth went dry and it was difficult to swallow. What could possibly be behind all those doors?

Somewhere down the corridor, a girl screamed. I froze, my body ice cold from fear.

A door squeaked open. Voices. I thought I recognized Mrs. Shadowford's voice, but she was too far away for me to understand what she was saying. But how had she gotten up here to the third floor in a wheelchair? The two figures forming in the distance were upright and walking. Then it couldn't be Mrs. Shadowford after all. Whoever it was, if they found me here, poking around where Ella Mae had specifically told me not to go, I would be in danger of getting kicked out of Shadowford.

My heart beat wildly in my chest. I couldn't let that happen. Not now, when I was just starting to figure this place out.

Quickly, I stepped back into the small room and closed the door. I walked down the narrow staircase to the second floor, through the secret doorway, and back to the safety of my bedroom.

IT TOTALLY WORKED

THURSDAY AFTERNOON, I sat on the wooden bleachers in the gym and listened as Mrs. King outlined the audition procedures. A panel of judges had been called in to watch us perform, including Brooke as captain of the squad and Mrs. King herself. Each girl would perform the cheers by herself, then all eight of us would perform the long dance as a group at the end of the auditions. Anyone who wanted to watch the auditions was welcome to sit in throughout the entire thing.

"Are you going to stay to watch everyone?" Agnes whispered. "I'm afraid it'll make me nervous if everyone else is like, crazy better than me, you know?"

I nodded, not taking my eyes off Mrs. King. My hand went to my throat where my mother's sapphire pendant was hidden underneath my t-shirt. I had spent a long time debating whether to wear the black diamond. It would pretty much guarantee me a spot on the squad, but at the same time, I would always know that I didn't earn it. Somehow, that didn't seem fair to Agnes and the other girls. I wanted to be a part of the team, but I wanted to really deserve it on my own merits.

Besides, I felt strange without my mother's pendant. It was probably just silly superstition, but I needed it.

Promise me you won't take it off.

A memory intruded on my thoughts. A boy's voice. Promise, he'd said.

"Harper Madison," Mrs. King said. I stood, my stomach filled with butterflies. "You're up."

I took in a deep breath and plastered a big smile across my face. I looked to Brooke for encouragement as I passed by the judges' table and she winked. I cleared my throat, threw my shoulders back, and jogged to the middle of the performance area.

The next hour passed by in a whirl of nerves and jittery excitement. I couldn't believe it! I'd done every single cheer perfectly! And when it came time for the dance, I knew I did my best. I kept my smile bright and tried to look confident. Basically, I nailed it.

"That was awesome," Brooke said once the tryouts were over and everyone filtered out of the gym. "What did I tell you about that diamond? It totally worked, right?"

"Yep," I said. I didn't want to tell her the truth. Let her think I was depending on their magic. I reached deep into my backpack and pulled out the blue velvet box. "Here. Thanks," I said. I bit my lip, wondering if I should just leave it at that.

"You are very welcome," she said.

I hesitated, then blurted out the question I'd been dying to ask her since I first realized what the black diamond had done for me. "How does it work? I mean, why does it work?"

Brooke smiled and looked around to make sure we were alone. "I can't really tell you," she said. "But if you make the squad, which I think you will, you'll be introduced to all kinds of things you never dreamed possible. Just you wait."

Excitement fluttered through me.

I'm counting on it.

THE NEW DEMONS
CHEERLEADER IS...

"*A*RE YOU PUMPED about the party tonight?" Drake put his arm around me and pulled me close. We were standing by my locker before calculus.

"I can't even think about the party yet," I said.

"Why not?"

"I'm too nervous about finding out whether I made the squad or not."

"From what I heard, you've got this," he said, kissing my forehead. He was so tall he towered over me. When I leaned in close, the top of my head barely reached his chin. "Mrs. King is making the announcement right after school?"

"Yep."

"Want me to come with you? For moral support?"

I smiled and looked up at him. "You'd do that?"

"Sure. No football practice on Fridays cause of the game tonight, so it's no problem. Maybe I can even give you a ride home afterward."

"That would be great, but what about Agnes? Ella Mae usually drives in to get us both. If I call to ask her if you can bring me home, she'll probably say no unless you want to take Agnes too."

He shrugged. "Whatever you want is fine with me. I just want to be close to you."

I blushed and leaned against his muscular chest. "Will you still feel that way if I don't make the squad?"

He laughed and squeezed me tighter, but he didn't say yes. A nervous knot formed in my stomach that didn't go away for the rest of the afternoon.

After the final bell, Drake and Brooke walked me to the gym. The current squad assembled on the floor with Mrs. King in front as the bleachers filled with students waiting to hear the announcement.

"Wow, there's a lot of people here," I said to Drake.

He squeezed my hand. "Everyone wants to see who the new cheerleader is. It's a really big deal here. I mean, Tori's death affected everyone. In a way, it's like filling her spot is a way of moving on."

I looked up at him, surprised he'd had such a deep insight. Maybe there was more to Drake Ashworth than I realized.

Agnes came up the stairs and sat down on my other side. "Hey," she said. "Nervous?"

"Extremely."

"Good luck," she said, crossing her fingers and holding them into the air.

"You too."

"Welcome everyone," Mrs. King began. "The death of Tori Fairchild was a tragedy for this community, and we know that no one can take her place in our hearts."

As she spoke, I couldn't help but wonder if her husband's relationship with Tori had been the reason she died. It was difficult to picture Mrs. King as a killer, but if she knew the truth about her husband and Tori, there was no telling what a powerful woman like her might be capable of.

"We also know that Tori would have wanted us to have the strongest squad possible for the rest of the games and competitions coming up this year. The sophomores that tried out yesterday did an amazing job, and I would like to thank each one of them for coming out this week and giving a hundred percent."

Everyone clapped politely. My right leg bounced up and down. Just tell us already.

"As you know, we do only have the one open slot, so even though competition was fierce, we can only invite one special girl to become a Demons cheerleader. And that girl is..."

I squeezed Drake's hand so hard his knuckles turned white. My breath caught in my chest, waiting to hear the name.

"Harper Madison!"

I jumped up and screamed, my face flushing with joy. Beside me, Agnes stood and gave me a big hug.

"Come on down and join us Harper," Mrs. King said.

The rest of the squad gathered around me, hugging me and telling me congratulations. Brooke pulled me out beside Mrs. King and lifted my hand into the air. The crowd in the gym was on their feet, whistling and cheering for me.

The moment was surreal. Was it really only a month ago that I had moved to Peachville? I never dreamed life could change so much so quickly.

My cheeks hurt from smiling so much as I waved to the crowd.

"Harper, we would like to present you with this brand new Demons uniform," Mrs. King said as Brooke handed me a blue and black sports bag that held my pom poms, shorts, a t-shirt with the Demon mascot, and a crisp new uniform. "Let's welcome Harper Madison to the team one more time!"

The crowd cheered and I scanned their faces. Movement to the right of the bleachers caught my eye and I turned to look. A handsome boy with brown spiked hair stood leaning against the wall, staring at me. The cheer of the crowd turned to background noise as our eyes met. For a moment, we were the only two in the room.

He lifted his chin in a nod of acknowledgment, then turned on his heel and left. I felt lightheaded and weak in the knees. I knew him from somewhere. But where? It seemed important.

Mrs. King's voice brought me out of my trance.

"Harper will be our honored guest tonight at the game and hopefully by next week, she'll be on the field cheering with us, so make sure y'all give her a warm welcome and lots of support over the next couple weeks. Go Demons!"

"GO DEMONS!" The squad yelled, then gathered me up in a group hug.

A NIGHT TO REMEMBER

*A*FTER THE ANNOUNCEMENT, Agnes and I walked to the parking lot together. Drake was waiting for us in his black Camaro. It was a sleek sports car his parents bought him as a present for his sixteenth birthday. It made me a little uncomfortable to think of riding around in such expensive cars in my torn jeans and old hand-me-downs.

Agnes climbed into the back.

"You sure you don't mind?" I said. "'Cause I could get in the back if you want."

"Don't be silly," she said. "I'm sure you want to ride up front with Drake."

I did, but I was desperately trying to be nice to her. I knew how much she wanted to be a Demons cheerleader. It was one of the first things she'd told me about herself when we met, and I had taken it from her.

Mrs. King only made me feel worse when she told Agnes that she was her second choice.

"At least that puts me in a good position for next year's auditions," Agnes had said. "Or if another spot opens up."

I didn't want to tell her that the chances of that happening were next to impossible.

As Drake spun out of the parking lot, he slipped in a CD. Rock music blasted out and he let down the windows. I was thankful for the music, because it meant we didn't have to worry about an awkward conversation that might make Agnes feel bad. I think Drake knew it, too. He looked over at me and winked.

At Shadowford, he got out of the car and walked me to the door. Agnes was about to go inside when he stopped her.

"You know, we're all having a party tonight at Foster's family's lake house," he said.

Agnes turned and lifted one eyebrow. "Are you talking to me?"

"Yeah," he said. "I know you're good friends with Harper, so if you want to come." He shrugged.

Her face lit up. "Seriously? That would be awesome, thanks. Can I ride with you guys?"

Drake glanced at me. "Sure," he said. "Bring a friend if you want. Or a boyfriend."

Agnes rolled her eyes. "I don't have a boyfriend, but I'm sure one of my friends'll come. I'm gonna go ask around. See ya tonight!"

She took off into the house. I smiled up at Drake.

"That was super sweet of you."

"Any friend of yours is a friend of mine," he said. "Besides, this is your night. We're going to have the best time ever."

He leaned down and brushed my lips lightly with his. As far as first kisses go, it wasn't bad. There was no movie music playing in the background. No crazy weak knees or fireworks shooting off inside my brain. But there was a stirring of butterflies. And butterflies are good.

"See you tonight," he said.

I smiled. "See you tonight."

When I saw him again, he was running onto the field with his teammates. As usual, Agnes and I were lined up with the rest of the fans as the team made their entrance. This time, though, Drake broke off from the team and came over to kiss my cheek.

The whole town came out to cheer on the Demons football team. To my great surprise, even Mrs. Shadowford came along to hear the announcement that one of her girls was chosen as the new cheerleader.

"I'm very proud of you, Harper," she said when I made it back up to the stands. "It's been a few years since one of my girls made the team."

"Who was the last one?"

She hesitated, as if trying to remember. "You know, I can't quite remember. I'd have to look it up."

I smiled at her, but in my gut, I felt that she was lying to me.

I thought about the picture of my mother and the other cheerleaders. Had my mother lived at Shadowford, too? Or any of the other women in the picture, like the mayor or the sheriff? I wondered. After what I'd seen on the third floor, I knew there had to be some connection between Shadowford and the magical power in this town. Hopefully now that I was an official member of the cheerleading squad, I would have access to some of those answers. I reminded myself to be patient. Answers would come in time. If I pushed too hard, the doors might close to me, and they would be a lot harder to get open a second time.

Just before halftime, the announcer called me down to join the other cheerleaders on the field. He introduced me to the crowd as the newest Demons cheerleader, and again I felt the heady rush of excitement and acceptance. The town welcomed me even though most of them had never even met me.

It should have been the happiest night of my life. And in some ways, it was. But there was always this feeling in the pit of my stomach that I was getting into something dangerous. As of today, I was a cheerleader. Girlfriend of the star quarterback.

One of the popular kids. It was exciting, but also terrifying. I had grown used to life as an outsider. I didn't know how to survive life on the inside of the circle. What if I couldn't handle it? What if I said the wrong thing or took a wrong turn?

Then again, I couldn't spend my entire life worrying about what might go wrong. So instead, I waved to the crowd and embraced my new existence.

Later, after the game was won, Agnes, Courtney and I all piled into Drake's car and headed out to the party.

"You were great out there tonight," I said to Drake.

He reached over and took my hand. "Thanks. I can't wait until you're on the field cheering for me." He glanced back to the girls in the backseat. "You guys ready to party?"

Agnes giggled. "This is so awesome," she said. "This will be my first official PHS party." She sounded excited.

"I am so ready to just let loose," Drake said. "Tonight, we can really celebrate Harper making the team."

"Yes," Agnes said. "Tonight is going to be a night to remember."

THEY CHOOSE YOU

RAKE DROVE THROUGH downtown, across a bridge, then out into the dark countryside beyond. I had never seen this side of town before.

"Where's this party anyway?"

He turned down the radio a bit. "Foster's parents have this cabin down by the lake. They let us use it whenever we want," he said. "It's completely stocked, too. You'll see."

Drake turned off the main highway onto a deserted dirt road. I couldn't see any lights and for a minute, I wondered if he'd gotten lost. Then, up ahead, a huge orange flame rose up.

"A bonfire?"

"So cool," Agnes said.

I didn't want to tell him how much fire scared me. Already, I could feel my palms getting sweaty. Great. Just what I needed.

At least thirty people were already dancing and drinking around the fire. A stereo system was set up on the huge side porch and the speakers blasted loud music. I wondered if there were any neighbors who might call and complain, then remembered that we were in the middle of nowhere. Plus, these were the rich kids. They probably never got in trouble.

The so-called cabin was actually more of a mansion. I figured anything over three thousand square feet lost the right to be labeled a cabin, but what did I know? Geez, what was it with this town and huge houses? This one raised up high into the sky, three stories up.

Drake's hand closed around mine and he led me through the party. I looked back to say something to Agnes, but she and Courtney had disappeared into the crowd. Oh well. I'd find them later.

Brooke, Allison, and Lark stood on the porch, their faces lit by firelight. They waved me over like we were old friends.

"Time for tequila," Brooke yelled over the music.

"Ew, I can't do it," Lark said. "I had the worst hangover last time. I think we should do a round of lemon drops in remembrance of Tori."

"Hell yeah," Allison said. "Lemon drops it is. You down, Harper?"

Everyone looked to me. What the hell. "Let's do this."

"I SERIOUSLY NEED to pee."

Lark grabbed my arm and practically dragged me toward the house. We'd been doing shots and dancing by the fire for the past hour, and to tell the truth, I'd had to pee for the last twenty minutes.

Together, we climbed our way through the crowd. Inside, though, both downstairs bathrooms had lines three people deep.

"Dammit, I'm going to seriously pee my pants," she said. She leaned against me and I struggled to hold her upright.

"If you pee on me, I swear to God, I'll never forgive you." I laughed and grabbed her hand. "Come on, let's check upstairs."

The second floor had several bedrooms. In the first room, a couple grunted in the shadows. "Taken," a guy yelled out. Lark and I giggled and shut the door.

A couple other rooms on that floor were locked tight, too.

"I think there's a third floor," I said.

Lark groaned. "You aren't seriously going to ask me to walk all the way up there?"

"Come on."

The stairs up to the third floor were dark and when I flipped the switch, nothing happened.

"Forget it," Lark said. "I'm going back down to wait."

"Scared of the dark?" I teased.

"Yes," she said. I laughed as she made her way back downstairs.

I wasn't scared of the dark. And I really needed to go to the bathroom. I didn't think I could wait for one to free up.

I slowly walked up to the third floor. From the second floor lights, I could tell that it was one big giant bedroom up here. A master suite? Sliding doors led out to a balcony with a view out toward the lake and a little bit of moonlight spilled in through the gauzy curtains. There had to be a bathroom up here somewhere.

I stumbled over a pillow and cursed, then laughed. Other than a glass of champagne I had sneaked at a party for one of my foster parent's twentieth wedding anniversaries, I had never drunk alcohol before. It made my head feel spinny and light.

I found the door to the bathroom and turned the knob, silently praying no one was in there. It opened easily and I ran my hand along the wall just inside the room. I flicked the light switch up, but again, nothing happened.

You've got to be kidding me.

I wasn't about to go back downstairs. I shut the door behind me, shutting out all light, and finally, happily, got rid of the pressure on my bladder. I giggled, thinking that Lark was probably still downstairs waiting in that line. All because she was afraid of a little darkness.

I washed my hands and stepped out into the large master suite.

A chill slid down my spine like an icy fingertip. Someone was in there with me. I could feel their energy. Their anger.

The hairs on my arms stood up and my breath caught in my throat. I felt instantly sober, all giddiness gone.

"Hello?" My voice came out a whisper.

A match struck and caught fire, lighting up a small area in the center of the room. Agnes sat on the carpet, holding a bright red candle. A pentagram was drawn around her with black sand.

"Agnes? What are you doing up here?" A knot formed in the pit of my stomach.

She didn't say a word. She sat the candle on the floor in front of her, and I stepped forward, thinking it would fall over on the carpet. Instead, the candle stayed upright. I wasn't even sure it was actually touching the floor at all.

I glanced toward the stairs, my legs tensing in case I needed to make a run for it.

"Congelo." Agnes' voice was commanding and deep. Not at all like her usual girly tone.

My legs felt suddenly stiff. I tried to step toward the stairs, but I couldn't move.

"You're not going anywhere," she said. The corners of her mouth raised up in a sinister smile that made my heart stop.

"What's going on?"

She threw back her head and laughed. "I'm making sure there's an extra opening on the cheerleading squad."

I felt sick.

"What have you done, Agnes?"

"I think you already know," she said, standing.

"It was you," I whispered. The image of Tori's half-burned body on the ground flashed through my memory. Oh, dear God,

I was going to be sick. I begged my legs to work, but I was frozen to the spot.

"I had the perfect plan," she said. "Get rid of one of the cheerleaders, then slip into her spot on the team. I knew they would hold auditions. Mrs. King isn't the type to miss out on an entire year of competitions and without a full team, the Demons would be disqualified."

"Why Tori?"

"Because I knew that when the police went searching for her killer, they would find several people who might want to get rid of her."

My mind struggled to understand what was going on. Agnes had killed Tori! And she had framed me for it. My hand went up to my sapphire pendant and Agnes laughed.

"Believe it or not, I picked Tori before you even moved to Peachville. Let's just say she had a secret relationship that provided a pretty clear motive for murder if the police needed someone to take the fall."

"Coach King," I whispered.

She raised one eyebrow and cocked her head to the side. "Wow, you knew about that too? Maybe you're smarter than I thought you were. Too bad that won't help you now."

I swallowed but my mouth had gone dry.

"Anyway, that was a tricky one because if Mrs. King ever found out I set her husband up, she might never let me on the squad." Agnes looked at me and smiled. "Then you moved in and gave me another idea."

"How could you do it?"

"What? Frame you? Or kill that blonde bitch who was never nice to anyone? It wasn't hard." Her hands rested by her side, and my eyes were drawn to them. Short crackles of light were coming from her fingertips like tiny sparks of electricity. "All I had to do was set you up to piss her off once or twice."

I remembered my first day of school when I had tripped and splattered ketchup all over Tori's shirt. I'd thought I tripped over a backpack or something, but when I had looked, there was nothing there. "You tripped me," I said.

"Very good," she said with a laugh. "Once everyone had seen you arguing with Tori, I just needed one more thing to seal your fate." She pointed toward my throat. "I saw that drawing you did of your mother. She was wearing the same necklace, so I knew it was important to you. Important enough that you would report it missing."

"All this just to be on the cheerleading squad? Are you crazy?"

Agnes drew in an angry breath. She lifted a finger toward me. Her hands were covered with a bright light of electric current. "You and I both know it's more than just a cheerleading squad. You don't even appreciate it half as much as I will," she said. Her voice was high and wild. "I don't understand why they picked you. After all the work I've done to learn how to control my power. I thought they would recognize my talents and reward me, but you..."

She raised both of her hands into the air. They were balls of light now, crackling with energy. I recognized that energy. For me, it manifested itself differently. I had no real control over the way objects moved when I got angry. Agnes, though, had learned to use and control her power.

"You are nothing," she said. Her feet rose off the ground and I gasped.

Outside, the music thumped. It was too loud. Even if I screamed, I knew no one would hear me.

"Being a Demons cheerleader is not just about competitions and dance routines and stupid football games," she said. "It's about being recruited. It's about being special enough that they are willing to hand you the keys that will help you unlock all of the magic inside. And instead of choosing me, the one with obvious power and potential, they choose you. An insignificant girl who has no idea how to cast a single spell."

Sparks shot out from her body in quick bursts. The sheriff had said Tori was burned, as if she'd been cooked from the inside. She had looked to me because of my history with fire, but it wasn't fire that killed Tori.

It was lightning.

A PART OF ME

FEAR RIPPED THROUGH my chest. I didn't want to die. For the first time in my life, I actually had something to live for. Something worth fighting for.

I stared down at the floating red candle and concentrated all of my anger onto it. At first, nothing happened. I felt helpless. Weak.

"When you're gone, Mrs. King will have to let me onto the squad," she said. "You heard her say that I was her second choice. Well, once everyone is finished mourning your death, I'll be her first choice. I figure it will take about a day for everyone to forget you. Or haven't you noticed that memory works a bit different here?"

Anger flared up inside me. In the center of the room, the red candle rose up higher, then with a flick of my hand, flew toward the curtains, lighting them on fire.

Agnes went into a rage. She turned her back to me and stepped out of the pentagram, desperately trying to put out the fire. Whatever spell she had cast that held my feet in place was released and I ran toward the stairs.

A stream of bright electric energy shot through the room and only missed me by inches as I jumped out of the way. Agnes moved quickly to block my exit. She'd been unable to put out the fire and flames engulfed that side of the room. Smoke filled the bedroom and I squinted to see. There had to be another way out.

Outside, the music stopped. Voices shouted from below, screams of fear.

"Not exactly the way I planned it," Agnes said. "But one way or another, you're not leaving this house alive."

She rose high into the air. Bright blue current ran up and down her body. Even her eyes glowed blue. I stepped back. She was too powerful for me. I didn't know the first thing about how to control my own power.

Her hand shot out and a bolt of energy flew at me. I didn't have time to jump out of the way. I lifted my hands to protect my face, bracing myself for the jolt of electricity. But it never came.

Agnes' eyes grew wide. She threw both hands out in front of her body. An arc of blue lightning shot out at me, but it dissipated before it connected. As though I were protected by an invisible force-field.

"What did you do?" she screamed.

I shook my head. I had no idea what was protecting me, but I didn't have a moment to waste. The fire was spreading rapidly. Smoke filled my lungs and I coughed, then crouched lower, searching for better air.

"We need to get out of here," I said.

Apparently, Agnes had no intention of letting me go. She roared and sent another bright shock of light across the room. This time, I felt a small jolt run through my body. It reminded me of the way it felt when you touched someone's hand and got shocked with static. Mild, but surprising. I jerked back, fear making my limbs weak.

I fell to my knees, the smoke becoming almost unbearable now. I heard a cackling, high-pitched laughter and looked up to see Agnes gathering a ball of light between her two hands.

"Goodbye Harper," she said.

My heartbeat roared in my ears. A memory came back to me in that instant. A drawing of a room full of flames. Jackson's voice.

This time the picture was different. This time you were wearing your necklace. Promise me you won't take it off, okay? No matter what.

I brought my hand up to my mother's necklace, then looked back at Agnes.

Just as she leaned back to throw her final bolt of lightning, a dark figure moved through the room. A figure bigger than a man, but partially transparent, like a shadow. It had the body of a gargoyle. A demon's face. I knew that whatever it was, it had come to protect me. I couldn't explain it, but when I saw the black shadow, I knew that it was a part of me.

The darkness circled around Agnes, and she screamed. It pulled her from the room. The glass of the sliding doors crashed as she broke through. Then, she disappeared behind a blanket of red flames.

A BEAUTIFUL DEMON

*A*S SOON AS Agnes disappeared into the fire, I ran for the stairs. My lungs burned from inhaling so much smoke, but I pushed my body to its limit. The flames consumed most of the top floor, and the two lower floors were lost in a sea of thick smoke. In the distance, I heard sirens wailing.

"Harper! Harper, where are you?" Drake's voice rose above the noise.

"Here," I tried to shout. Instead, my voice came out cracked and dry. I coughed and fell to my knees on the second floor landing.

I forced myself up again, grabbing the banister and pulling myself down the stairs. The overhead lights on the first floor cut through some of the smoke. I saw Drake's tall form rushing back and forth, and I reached out to him.

"Harper?"

My hands circled up around his neck just as my legs gave out again. Drake lifted me into his arms and carried me from the house. Outside, the bonfire was going strong, but no one was dancing or cheering. Everyone was backed up across the street from the cabin, their horror-stricken faces watching as Foster's house burned to the ground.

"Agnes," I said. "Where's Agnes? We have to make sure-"

Drake put a hand over my mouth. "It's going to be okay, Harper. Don't talk. Be still."

I struggled, my mind racing. She would come for me. Agnes wasn't going to stop until I was dead. Drake carried me across to the other side of the road and laid me down in the grass. I tried to stand, looking back toward the burning house to see if I could find her.

That's when I noticed a flash of bright red on the ground in front of the house. My mouth fell open. Agnes lay in a crumpled heap beneath the third floor balcony, her body broken and still. When the fire department arrived, the paramedics pronounced her dead at the scene. Later, authorities theorized that she must have gone into a panic when flames trapped her up on the third floor. She broke through the locked balcony door and jumped to her death to avoid burning alive.

It would be a long time before I told anyone the truth about what really happened to Agnes that night.

I was in the back of the ambulance breathing in oxygen from a face mask when Mrs. King came rushing around the corner to see if I was alright. A blanket was wrapped around my body to shield me from the night air.

"Thank goodness," she said, placing her hand over her heart. There were tears in her eyes. "I don't know what we would have done if we'd lost you."

Her emotion touched my heart. I tried to smile, but my entire body ached from exhaustion. She climbed into the back of the ambulance with me and asked the paramedic if she could have a moment alone with me.

"You have no idea just how special you are to us." She stroked my hair gently and put her arm around me.

"Agnes-" I said, then began to cough again.

Mrs. King pulled the oxygen mask from my hand. Confused, I took in a shallow breath. She placed her palm flat against my chest and closed her eyes. My body began to hum and tingle, and I felt a warm energy flow through me.

"Breathe," she said.

I took a deep, cleansing breath and felt no urge to cough. "How...?"

She smiled and brushed a strand of hair off my face. "Shhh," she whispered. "All of your questions will be answered, I promise. But you need to be patient."

Patience is a hard thing when there are so many unanswered questions. I opened my mouth to ask just one, but she placed her palm against my forehead.

"Rest," she said. "I need you at a hundred percent, okay?"

I nodded, feeling suddenly very sleepy. My lungs no longer hurt, though, and that was very good.

Mrs. King pulled the blanket up to my chin and smiled.

"You're going to make a beautiful Demon."

ABOUT SARRA—

 Sarra Cannon writes contemporary and paranormal fiction with both teen and college aged characters. Her novels often stem from her own experiences growing up in the small town of Hawkinsville, Georgia, where she learned that being popular always comes at a price and relationships are rarely as simple as they seem.

She has sold over a quarter of a million books since she first began her career as an Indie author in 2010.

Sarra is a devoted (obsessed) fan of Hello Kitty and has an extensive collection that decorates her desk as she writes. She currently lives in South Carolina with her amazingly supportive husband and her adorable son.

Connect with Sarra online!
Website: SarraCannon.com
Facebook: Facebook.com/sarracannon
Instagram: instagram.com/sarracannon
Twitter: twitter.com/sarramaria
Goodreads: Goodreads.com/Sarra_Cannon

Made in the USA
Lexington, KY
02 June 2015